# THE
# NIGHT
# WALKER

Also by Sebastian Fitzek

*The Child*

# THE
# NIGHT
# WALKER

## SEBASTIAN FITZEK

Translated by Jamie Lee Searle

sphere

SPHERE

First published in the English language in
Great Britain in 2016 by Sphere
Originally published in German as *Der Nachtwandler*
in 2013 by Droemer Knaur

1  3  5  7  9  10  8  6  4  2

This book is published by agreement with AVA International GmbH,
Germany (www.ava-international.de)

A CIP catalogue record for this book
is available from the British Library.

ISBN 978-0-7515-5683-4

Typeset in Sabon by Palimpsest Book Production Limited,
Falkirk, Stirlingshire
Printed and bound in Great Britain by Clays Ltd, St Ives plc

Papers used by Sphere are from well-managed forests
and other responsible sources.

MIX
Paper from
responsible sources
FSC® C104740

Sphere
An imprint of
Little, Brown Book Group
Carmelite House
50 Victoria Embankment
London EC4Y 0DZ

An Hachette UK Company
www.hachette.co.uk

www.littlebrown.co.uk

For Manuela

By a route obscure and lonely,
Haunted by ill angels only,
Where an Eidolon, named NIGHT,
On a black throne reigns upright,
I have wandered home but newly
From this ultimate dim Thule.

'Dream-Land', Edgar Allan Poe

# Prologue

The patient hadn't even been on the ward for half an hour, and already he was causing trouble. Sister Susan had *tasted* it, almost as soon as the ambulance opened its doors and the stretcher was pushed out.

She could always taste it when problems rolled into the psychiatric department. She would get this strange sensation in her mouth, as though she was chewing on aluminium foil. It could even be unleashed by patients who at first glance seemed more like victims and not aggressive in the slightest; much like the man who had just activated the alarm in Room 1310.

*And at five to eight, of all times.*

If he could just have waited another five minutes, Susan would have been on her break. Instead, she had to rush along the corridor on an empty stomach. Not that she had much of an appetite in the evenings anyway. She took great care not to gain weight, even though she wasn't much bigger than some of the anorexia patients being treated on the ward. The tiny salad and half an egg were part of her evening routine – as was, admittedly, a paranoid schizophrenic with hallucinations, but she would have gladly relinquished the latter.

The patient had been found lying naked in the snow

outside a supermarket, covered in blood and with lacerations on his feet. He had appeared bedraggled, disorientated and dehydrated, but his gaze was alert and steady, his voice clear, and his teeth (teeth, as far as Susan was concerned, were always a sure indication of the state of the soul) showed no signs of alcohol, nicotine or substance abuse.

*And yet I could still taste it*, she thought, with one hand on her bleeper and the other on her bunch of keys.

Susan unlocked the door and entered the room.

The scene before her was so bizarre that she stood in shock for a moment before pressing the bleeper to call the security team, who were trained especially for situations such as these.

'I can prove it,' screamed the naked man in front of the window. He was standing in a pool of vomit.

'Of course you can,' answered the sister, taking care to keep her distance.

Her words sounded rehearsed rather than genuine, because Susan had indeed rehearsed them and didn't intend them to be genuine, but in the past she had often been able to win time with empty platitudes.

Not this time, though.

Later, in its final report, the inquiry panel would establish that the cleaning woman had been listening to music on an MP3 player, something strictly forbidden during working hours. When her supervisor came by unexpectedly to do a hygiene check, she had hidden the device in the water meter cupboard next to the shower.

But in the moment of crisis it was a mystery to Sister Susan how the patient had come into possession of the electronic device. He had ripped open its battery compartment and was holding a bent alkaline battery, which he must have chewed open with his teeth. Although Susan couldn't actually see it, she pictured the viscous battery acid flowing over the edges like marmalade.

'Everything's going to be OK,' she said, trying to placate him.

'No, nothing's going to be OK,' the man protested. 'Listen to me. I'm not crazy. I tried to throw up to get it out of my stomach, but maybe I've already digested it. Please. You have to take an X-ray. You have to X-ray my body. The proof is inside me!'

He screamed and screamed until, eventually, the security team came in and restrained him.

But they were too late. By the time the doctors rushed into the room, the patient had long since swallowed the battery.

# A few days before

Somewhere in the world.
In a town you know.
Maybe even in your neighbourhood . . .

# 1

The cockroach was creeping towards Leon's mouth.

Just another few centimetres and its long feelers would touch his open lips. It had already reached the fleck of drool he had left on the bed-sheet in his sleep.

Leon tried to close his mouth, but his muscles were paralysed.

*It's happening again.*

He couldn't get up, raise his hand or even blink. He had no choice but to stare at the cockroach, which was lifting up its wings as if extending some friendly greeting:

*Hello, Leon, I'm back. Don't you recognise me?*

*Yes, of course I do. I know exactly who you are.*

They had christened it Morphet, the gigantic cockroach from Réunion. He hadn't realised that these repulsive things could actually fly. When they looked on the internet afterwards they found all these crazy discussion threads on the topic, and from that day on they were able to add their own unequivocal contribution: cockroaches from Réunion were certainly able to, and it must have been one of these flight-enabled specimens that Natalie had brought back from holiday nine months ago. The monstrosity must have crawled into her suitcase while she was packing, and when she opened the case back at home, Morphet had been sat there on her dirty washing, cleaning his feelers. Natalie hadn't even had time to draw breath to scream before the cockroach flew off, hiding itself in some unreachable corner of the old building.

They had searched everywhere. Every nook and cranny, of which there were many in the high-ceilinged rooms of their three-bedroom apartment: under the skirting boards, behind the washer-dryer in the bathroom, among Leon's architectural models in his study – they even turned the dark room upside down, despite the fact that Natalie had sealed the door to her photography lab with light-excluding material and always kept it locked. But it was all in vain. The gigantic insect with its spider-like legs and bluebottle-coloured shell could not be found.

On that first night Natalie seriously contemplated leaving the apartment they had moved into only a few months before.

*The apartment where we wanted to make a fresh start.*

Later, after having sex, they had laughingly reassured one another that Morphet was sure to have flown out of the window to the park, to discover that those of his kind in this town were a little smaller and less hairy than he was.

*But now he's back.*

Morphet was so close now that Leon could *smell* him. Nonsense, of course, but his disgust at the cockroach was so great that Leon's senses were playing tricks on him. He was even convinced he could make out on its hairy legs the faecal remains of the countless dust mites it had hoarded beneath the bed under the cloak of darkness. Its feelers still hadn't made contact with Leon's dry, open lips, but he already thought he could feel the tickling sensation. And he had a premonition of how it would feel when the cockroach crept into his mouth. It would be salty and scratchy, like popcorn when it clings to your palate.

Then Morphet would slowly but surely force himself into Leon's throat, bashing his wings against his teeth along the way.

*And I can't even bite.*

Leon groaned, trying with all his might to scream.

Sometimes it helped, but it usually took more than that to free himself from the sleep paralysis.

He knew, of course, that the cockroach wasn't real. It was early in the morning, a few days before New Year, and pitch black in the bedroom. It was physically impossible to see even his hand right in front of his face, but none of these certainties made the horror any more bearable. Because disgust, even at its most intense, is never material, but instead a psychological reaction to some external influence. Whether this influence is imagined or really exists makes no difference at all to how it feels.

*Natalie!*

Leon tried to scream his wife's name, but failed miserably. Just as so many times before, he was imprisoned in a waking nightmare from which he couldn't escape without help.

*People with ego weakness are particularly prone to sleep paralysis,* Leon had once read in a popular psychology magazine, partly recognising himself in the article. Although he didn't have an inferiority complex as such, he secretly saw himself as a 'Yes, but' person: yes, his dark hair was full and thick, but its numerous kinks ensured that he tended to look as though he had just fallen out of bed. Yes, his chin and its gently sloping V-shape might give his face an attractively masculine appearance, but his beard resembled that of a teenager. Yes, he had white teeth, but when he laughed too hard you could see that his fillings had paid for his dentist's SUV. And yes, he was six feet tall, but seemed shorter on account of the fact that he never stood up straight. In brief: he wasn't bad looking. But women who were looking for a good time, even though they may have given him a smile, never gave him their telephone numbers. They gave them to his best friend Sven instead, who had been blessed with a royal flush in the game of genetic poker: great hair, teeth, lips, a strong build . . . everything like Leon, except without the 'but'.

*Natalie?* Grunting, Leon tried to fight his way out of the paralysis. *Please help me. Morphet is about to crawl across my tongue.*

He was taken aback by the unexpected sound coming from his mouth. Even when dreaming, he only ever spoke, grunted or cried out in his own, familiar voice. But the whimper he was hearing now sounded softer, higher. More like the voice of a woman.

'Natalie?'

All at once it became light in the room.

*Thank God.*

This time he had managed to free himself from the clutches of his nightmare without kicking and screaming. He knew that at some point in their life most people would suffer from the same thing, imprisoned in the shadowy world between sleeping and waking. A world you could only escape with the greatest strength of will. Or through some para-doxical disturbance from the outside. If someone turned on a bright light in the middle of the night, for example, or if loud music was playing, or if an alarm started or . . . *if someone was crying?*

Leon pulled himself upright and blinked.

'Natalie?'

His wife was kneeling in front of the wardrobe opposite the bed with her back to him. She seemed to be looking for something among her shoes.

'Sorry, sweetheart, did I wake you?'

No response, just a long-drawn-out sob. Natalie sighed, then the whimper quietened down.

'Are you OK?'

She silently pulled a pair of ankle boots from the cupboard and threw them into . . .

. . . *her suitcase?*

Leon flung back the blanket and got out of bed.

'What's wrong?' He looked at the clock on his nightstand. It was only a quarter to seven. So early that not even the light in Natalie's aquarium had come on.

'Are you still angry?'

They had argued repeatedly throughout the whole of the previous week, and two days ago things had escalated. Both of them were so busy at work that they could barely see straight. She had her first big photography exhibition looming, and he was preparing for the architecture pitch. Each had accused the other of neglect, and each thought their own commitments the most important.

On Christmas Eve the word 'divorce' had been uttered for the first time, and even though neither of them meant it seriously, it was an alarming sign of how raw their nerves were. Yesterday Leon wanted to extend an olive branch by taking Natalie out for a reconciliation dinner, but she'd come home late from the gallery yet again.

'Listen, I know we have our problems at the moment, but—'

She spun around to face him and the sight of her hit him like a blow to the gut.

'Natalie, what—' He blinked, wondering if he could still be dreaming. 'What the hell happened to your face?'

The skin around her right eye was deep violet and her eyelids were swollen shut. She was dressed, but it looked like she had thrown everything on in a rush. The flower-patterned blouse with the ruffled sleeves was buttoned up

11

unevenly, her trousers were missing the belt, and the laces of her high-heeled suede boots were flapping around loose.

She turned away from him again. Moving awkwardly, she tried to close the suitcase, but it was too small for all the things she'd tried to cram into it. A red silk slip, a scarf and her favourite white skirt bulged out of the sides.

Leon moved closer and went to pull her into his arms in a reassuring embrace, but Natalie flinched away in fear.

'What's wrong with you?' he asked in confusion as she hastily reached for her suitcase. Four of her fingernails were painted a mud-like colour. The thumbnail was missing.

'Jesus Christ, your thumb!' cried Leon, trying to grab her injured hand. Then the sleeve of Natalie's blouse slid upwards and he saw the cuts.

*From a razor blade?*

'For the love of God, Natalie. Have you started with that again?'

'Me?'

It was the first question he had asked that actually prompted an answer.

In her gaze was a mix of bewilderment, fear and – the most confusing thing to Leon right now – pity. She had opened her lips by only a narrow slit, but it was enough to see that a large part of one of her front teeth was missing.

'*Me?*'

He froze in shock, and Natalie pulled herself free from his touch. She grabbed her mobile from the bed. Her good-luck charm swung from the smartphone, a pink artificial-pearl chain on which each bead was decorated with a letter from her name – Natalie's name band, which had been fastened on to her wrist in the hospital the day she was born twenty-seven years ago. With her suitcase in the other hand, she rushed across the room.

'Where are you going?' he cried, but she was already half out the door. He tried to run into the hallway after her, but stumbled over a crate of building plans that he had been going to take into the office.

'Natalie, please just explain to me . . .'

She ran down the steps, not turning around to him even once.

Later, in the days of horror that followed, Leon was no longer sure if it was his imagination or if his wife really had been dragging her right leg as she hurried to the door. Although it could equally have been because of the suitcase, or the fact that her shoes weren't properly fastened.

Once Leon had picked himself up again, she had disappeared into the ancient lift and had pulled the manual door across in front of her like a protective shield. The last thing he saw of his wife, the woman he had shared the last three years of his life with, was that horrified, fearful (and pitiful?) gaze: *'Me?'*

The lift began to move. After standing there for an instant, frozen in shock, Leon ran to the stairs.

The wide wooden steps, coiling their way downwards around the lift shaft like a snake, were covered with sisal carpet, the coarse fibres of which pricked the soles of his feet. Leon was wearing nothing but a loose pair of boxer shorts, which were threatening to slip down over his slim hips with every step he took.

Taking several steps at a time, he reckoned he could reach the ground floor in time. Then old Ivana Helsing on the second floor opened her apartment door, admittedly only by a crack and without taking off the safety chain from the inside, but it was still enough to break Leon's rhythm.

'Alba, come back,' he heard his neighbour calling out, but it was too late. The black cat had slipped out of the apartment into the stairway, running between his legs. So as not to fall flat on his face, he had to grab on to the handrail with both hands and bring himself to a halt.

'Good God, Leon! What's wrong?'

He ignored the concerned voice of the elderly woman, who had now opened her door completely and stepped out. He pushed his way past.

There was still time. He could hear the creaking of the lift's wooden cabin and the crackling of the steel cable from which it was hanging.

Arriving on the ground floor, he veered around the corner, slid across the smooth marble and ended up huddled on all fours, wheezing and panting, in front of the lift door. The cabin slowly sunk down to rest in its standby position.

And then . . . nothing.

No rattling or clattering, no sound at all to indicate someone was about to get out.

'Natalie?'

Leon took a deep breath, pulled himself to his feet and tried to peer through the colourful art nouveau stained-glass panes set into the door, but all he could see were shadows.

So he opened the door from the outside. Only to find himself staring at his own reflection.

The mirrored cabin was empty; Natalie had gone. Vanished.

How was that possible?

Leon looked around in search of help, and at that moment Dr Michael Tareski came into the empty hallway. The chemist – who lived above Leon on the fourth floor, never greeted him and always looked listless – was wearing a tracksuit and trainers instead of his usual blazer and white linen trousers. A glistening brow and dark flecks around the armpits of his sweatshirt betrayed the fact that he had just been for an early-morning run.

'Have you seen Natalie?' asked Leon.

'Who?'

Tareski's wary gaze wandered from Leon's naked torso down to his boxer shorts. Presumably the chemist was running through a mental list of the medication that could be responsible for his neighbour's confused state. Either that, or the ones that could put him right again.

'Oh, you mean your wife?' Tareski turned away and went over to the mailboxes on the wall, which meant that Leon could no longer see his face as he replied: 'She just left in a taxi.'

Feeling dazed, Leon scrunched up his eyes as if blinded by the beam of a torch, then went past Tareski to the main door.

'You'll catch your death out there,' the chemist warned him, and as Leon opened the door and stepped out on to the stone steps leading down to the pavement every muscle in his body cramped up in agreement. The building was in a reduced traffic zone in the old town, with lots of boutiques, restaurants, cafés, theatres and art-house cinemas like the Celeste, the malfunctioning neon sign of which was flickering on to the neighbouring house above Leon's head in the early-dawn light.

The antique-looking street lights, modelled on gas lanterns, were still burning. At this hour on a weekend very few people were around. In the distance a man was walking his dog, and opposite a man was just pulling up the shutters of his newspaper kiosk. But most people weren't even awake yet, let alone out and about. This year the Christmas holidays had fallen so that just a few days of holiday had been enough to bridge the time until the New Year's celebrations. The streets looked abandoned, whichever direction Leon looked. No cars, no taxis, no Natalie.

His teeth began to chatter, and he wrapped his arms around his upper body. By the time he stepped back into the shelter of the lobby, Tareski had disappeared into the lift.

Shivering with cold, confused, and unwilling to wait, Leon took the stairs instead.

This time no cat ran across his path. Ivana Helsing's door was closed, even though Leon felt sure the old woman was watching him through the peephole. Just like the Falconis on the first floor, the childless, melancholic couple who he was sure to have woken with his stumbling and clamouring.

It was very likely they would make another complaint about him to the building management, just like they had when he celebrated his twenty-eighth birthday rather too loudly back in the spring.

Confused, exhausted and trembling all over, Leon reached the third floor, thankful the door was still ajar and he hadn't locked himself out. Natalie's perfume, a subtle summery scent, still hung in the air. For a moment he lost himself in the hope that he had just dreamed it all, that the woman he wanted to spend the rest of his life with would still be sleeping peacefully, wrapped up in the thick quilt. But then he saw Natalie's untouched side of the bed, and knew his wish would not be granted.

He stared at the ransacked wardrobe, the lower drawer of which was still open. It was empty, as was the small bureau next to the window which, until yesterday, housed her make-up brushes. Now it held only the laptop they watched DVDs on now and again. A compromise, because Natalie hadn't wanted a TV in the bedroom.

The clock on Leon's nightstand jumped to 7 a.m., and the fluorescent lamps above the tall aquarium flickered on. Leon saw his reflection in the shimmering, green-tinged glass of the tank. There was no longer even a single fish swimming in the four hundred litres of fresh water.

Three weeks before, all the angel fish had perished due

to a persistent fungus, even though Natalie had tended to her precious possessions meticulously, checking the water quality on a daily basis. She was so despondent afterwards that Leon had doubted she would ever keep fish again.

The autotimer was still set only because, over the years, they had got used to being woken by the light of the aquarium. Leon angrily pulled the electricity cable out of the plug socket. The light extinguished, and he felt lost.

He sat down on the edge of the bed, buried his head in his hands and tried to find an innocent explanation for what had just happened. But as hard as he tried, he was unable to suppress the certainty that, despite all the doctors' protestations that he had been cured, the past had caught up with him again.

His illness had come back.

# 2

'. . . you have to speak into it.'

'Into what?'

'For heaven's sake – into the telephone, of course!'

The older man on the tape sounded impatient; it clearly wasn't the first time he had tried to explain to his wife how to record an answerphone message. The line crackled, then it seemed that Leon's mother had brought the receiver into the correct position.

'You have reached the home of Klaus and Maria Nader,' she said, sounding like someone who was doing a bad imitation of a satnav.

*Please turn around at the next available opportunity.*

'Unfortunately we're not here right now.'

'Speak for yourself,' interjected his father drily from the background.

Even though Leon wasn't in the mood, having felt sick and numb all morning, he couldn't help but chuckle. His adoptive parents didn't miss a single opportunity to act like the old couple on the balcony in *The Muppet Show*. With or without an audience, at home or out in public, barely a sentence from one of them failed to draw commentary from the other. Unwitting onlookers often thought they were witnessing the final scenes of a marriage in its death throes. But that couldn't have been further from the truth.

'And we won't be able to return your call for a while, either, because we're on a cruise,' explained Maria on the tape.

'Why don't you just say where any potential thieves can find the house keys while you're at it?'

'And what would they take? Your Caracho railway?'

Leon smiled.

His mother knew, of course, that the brand was Carrera; she said it wrong on purpose to annoy Klaus. The racing circuit in the loft was his pride and joy. Klaus Nader had always played with it at Christmas, while Leon had only been allowed to watch. At most now and again he had been permitted to put back one of the race cars that had fallen off, while his old man operated the speed control with his eyes glistening. It was a father-and-son classic.

Klaus had more time for his hobby now that the arthritis in his knuckle had rendered him unable to stay in his job as a waiter, much to Maria's chagrin, who now had to 'put up with the old dog' at home all day.

*God, I miss them*, thought Leon wistfully. He would have given anything to be able to talk to them in person right now. Once again it was far too long since they had last seen each other.

He closed his eyes and longed to be back at the head of the narrow wooden table in the kitchen, the best seat in the Naders' end-of-terrace house for watching their affectionate bickering. Leon could picture his father clearly: his shirt-sleeves rolled up, his broad elbows on the table as he rubbed his chin thoughtfully, waiting for the scrambled eggs that his wife was preparing for him.

*If it takes any longer I'm going to need another shave already.*

*Good idea, and why don't you do your back while you're at it?*

*Are you trying to imply I have a hairy back?*

*Of course not. Just like you don't have a double chin.*

*What are you talking about? I just have a few wrinkles on my neck, not a double chin.*

*That's what I said.*

'Our son bought us the cruise as a present,' Maria announced proudly on the answerphone.

'He's such a good boy,' murmured Klaus, quoting one of Maria's favourite commentaries, which she always had at the ready whenever someone mentioned her son.

'He sure is. And there's no need to roll your eyes like that, you old fool—'

A beeping tone then accomplished something that Klaus Nader only rarely managed. It silenced Maria, reminding Leon of the reason for his call.

'Er, Mama, Papa?' he said, feeling flustered. 'Nice message. I'm just calling because I . . .'

*. . . wanted to ask if Natalie has been in touch with you?*

It had been the same for his parents as it had for him. They'd fallen in love with Natalie the very second they met her.

'Call me shallow,' his father had said, taking him to the side briefly after Natalie had left the garden that summer afternoon to help Maria with the salad in the kitchen, 'but if the contents are even half as beautiful as the packaging with this woman, then you'll be even more of a loon than the idiot who messed up the fifty-euro question on *Who Wants to be a Millionaire?* yesterday if you ever let her go.'

The affection was mutual, for Natalie had doted on the cranky couple. Especially Maria, which was astonishing when you thought about it, because the two women could hardly be more different.

Natalie wanted to pursue her career as a photographer

and travel the world as a celebrated artist, while Maria was a housewife who saw the legacy she would bequeath to the world in Leon, not in a retrospective at the Guggenheim Museum. She wore her apron as proudly as Natalie did her stilettos. And while Natalie Lené had grown up in a twenty-room villa, Maria Nader had spent her childhood literally on the street, in a motorhome with a retractable awning and a chemical toilet.

The thing that united these two very different women was not their past or their plans for the future, but the fact that both were judged incorrectly by those around them. Natalie wasn't a superficial bimbo any more than Maria was a simple-minded housewife. They were just two people on the same wavelength; it was up to other people if they wanted to waste their valuable time on earth wondering how such an affinity was possible.

They trusted one another, and so it was very possible that Natalie had turned to Maria in her moment of need. But despite this, Leon had made the phone call without holding out any great hopes, and only now, a day after her hurried departure.

Yesterday he had spent hours waiting for a call that would put his mind at rest, and the countless times he had dialled Natalie's mobile number he had only reached the voicemail.

Today, still not having received a sign of life from her, he was tentatively beginning to contact people he could trust. People Natalie might confide in.

But he had stumbled into a dead end. His parents were away. On the high seas. Unreachable.

*Like Natalie.*

Leon realised that he had said nothing for too long, that for the last few seconds the answerphone would have picked up only his breathing, if that. Feeling dazed, he hung up without saying goodbye.

If his parents listened to the abrupt message after their return, they would be sure to call him back right away.

But Leon doubted they could ever feel as distressed as he did right now.

He didn't know what had happened to Natalie, or why she had left him so hurriedly. Leon knew only one thing: whatever his parents might think, he had never given them a cruise as a present.

# 3

'Did I wake you?'

'Does size matter?' grumbled the voice at the other end. 'Of course you woke me, you idiot.'

'I'm sorry,' Leon apologised to Anouka.

She was Natalie's best friend and, for that reason, the second person on the list of trusted confidants to contact. It was just before nine in the morning, but Anouka was known for being a night owl, and never made an appearance in the gallery before noon. He was sure to have torn her from a deep sleep. Or from the arms of one of the numerous lovers she regularly picked up in the clubs of the city.

Leon couldn't totally understand her success with men, but then again beauty was known to lie in the eye of the beholder. The men drawn to Natalie's svelte girlish body, her long dark hair and melancholic gaze had very little in common with the muscle-bound, hairy-chested and – at first glance – somewhat jaded men who tended to ogle Anouka's artificially enhanced breasts in karaoke bars.

'You sound strange,' Anouka commented. He heard the rustle of bed-sheets, then the sound of bare feet padding across parquet flooring.

'Have you taken something?'

'Don't be ridiculous.'

'Has something happened?'

Leon hesitated. 'I . . . I was hoping you might be able to tell me.'

'Eh?'

'Is Natalie with you?'

'Why would you think that?'

Leon felt sure he could hear water gurgling, and if he knew Natalie's best friend as well as he thought he did, she was squatting on the toilet right now and urinating unashamedly while he was on the line.

'It's complicated. I'm kind of out of sorts, but I don't want to talk about it now, OK?'

'You don't want to talk about it but you called me in the middle of the night?' Anouka managed to inject both amusement and annoyance into her tone at the same time. The sound of a toilet flushing thundered down the line.

'Natalie left the apartment yesterday, and I haven't been able to reach her since,' explained Leon, turning towards the living-room door. He had been pacing up and down between the sofa and the window while talking, but his throat was beginning to tickle, so he decided to get a glass of water from the kitchen.

'Did you have an argument?' asked Anouka.

'I don't know.'

'You don't know whether or not you had an argument?'

*I don't even know if it might have been something much worse than a harmless argument, but you would never understand that.*

'This must sound really strange, I know, but could you please do me a favour and tell her to call me if you see her in the gallery today?'

Natalie and Anouka had shared first a room and then an apartment during art college. Long before Natalie met Leon, the two women had pledged to realise their dream of opening their own photography gallery in the old town. A space where they would exhibit their own pictures, along with those of other young artists. About a year ago they had put the dream into action and, following the first few press reviews, the gallery had got off to a great start.

'I can't,' said Anouka.

'You can't what?'

'Ask her to call you.'

'Sorry?'

He knew Anouka had hated him ever since Natalie moved out of their apartment together to live with him. She saw him as a bourgeois stiff, because his work as an architect was commercial rather than artistic. On the rare occasions when they met up, they exchanged the bare minimum of small talk, and the aversion had been mutual ever since Leon found out that Anouka had begged her girlfriend not to get into a relationship with him. But despite all the antipathy, until today she had never acted in a hostile way towards him, at least not openly.

'You don't want to give her my message?'

'No, I *can't*, because it's likely I won't see her.'

'What's that supposed to mean?'

'It means your darling Natalie hasn't come to work for the last two weeks. I'm running the gallery all by myself.'

Stunned, as though Anouka had just dealt him a blow to the head, he came to an abrupt halt in the hallway and stared at the magnetic board fastened to the closed kitchen door at head height. Natalie and he used to leave each other affectionate, playful messages on it, depending on who left the house first in the morning. But the last one (*Sweetheart, did we have sex last night? Sorry if I snored. Nat*) had been months ago, and now there was just a notice from the building administration under the magnet, announcing to residents that the renovation of the stairway would begin in a few days' time. (*Be prepared for long waits for the lift!*)

'But Natalie told me you two were working on a big exhibition?'

*Star Children.*

An exhibition of images as moving as they were disturbing, on the subject of miscarriages and still-births.

*That, after all, was why Natalie had been leaving early in the morning and coming back late at night.*

Just like the day before yesterday!

He had waited for her in the dining room with a bottle of conciliatory wine, eventually opening it as the evening turned to night. Once it was empty, he had fallen into bed drunk, not even noticing how or when Natalie arrived home.

'She told me you guys were working flat out to get everything ready in time.'

'Flat out is right. But I'm doing it all by myself, Leon. I've got no idea what's going on with her. I know she can be a bit unreliable at times, but not calling me back one single time even though I've left dozens of messages on her phone, that's a bit much even for her. I mean, the exhibition was her idea, but perhaps it was too soon.'

*No, I don't believe that.*

After the miscarriage last summer, Natalie had been devastated, but she got over it with astonishing speed. Perhaps because it happened in the tenth week, together with her period, meaning that a scrape wasn't necessary.

*A star child.*

He had been so happy when her period didn't come. She hadn't told him about the first signs – the soreness in her breasts, the sensitivity to smell first thing in the morning – from fear it could turn out to be a false alarm. But then she bought a test, and those few days after the positive result were the most wonderful of his life.

Then came the morning when she discovered the blood in her pants, and their plans evaporated into thin air, along with the joyful anticipation. It was awful, but somehow, after a short, intensive period of grief, the incident ended up bringing them even closer together. If he hadn't had this feeling, he wouldn't have proposed to her two months ago.

*And she had said yes!*

The wedding was rather unorthodox; without any witnesses, a photographer or flower girls. They had simply picked the first available appointment at the registry office. Many of their friends reacted with surprise, and some were even indignant, but why shouldn't they get married in exactly the same way as they fell in love: head over heels?

'She was over the worst of it,' said Leon, more to himself than Anouka.

Remembering that he wanted a glass of water, he opened the kitchen door, then began to cough.

Something in the air was making it almost impossible to enter the room. It felt like thick smoke, but the substance irritating his throat and forcing tears to his eyes in a matter of seconds was completely invisible.

'What did you say?' asked Anouka.

'Nothing,' he spluttered, rushing over to the kitchen window with his hand pressed against his mouth. He flung it open and sucked the cold, clear air into his lungs with relief.

'Anyway, Leon. Whatever's going on at home with you two doesn't really have anything to do with me. I was actually hoping that *you* might call to explain why Natalie's been so rattled recently.'

Leon rubbed his eyes, turning round and searching for the source of the irritant. His gaze fell on the microwave, the neon display of which was blinking.

'I mean, she decides to give up now, of all the moments

she could choose. We're still in the beginning stages, we made a profit for the very first time last month, and now Natalie throws in the towel. I just don't get it.'

*Nor do I*, thought Leon, opening the microwave and starting to cough again. He had found the origin of the acrid smell.

'Is everything OK?' asked Anouka.

*No. Nothing, nothing at all, is OK.*

With his fingertips, he reached for the trainers in the microwave, but was unable to lift them. The rubber soles had melted on to the microwave plate, and the sight awakened a memory of a time that Leon had so far regarded to be the worst in his life.

Without saying goodbye, he hung up on Anouka and hurried out of the kitchen, along the hallway and into his study. He had to lift up the cardboard model of the children's hospital, which the architectural firm had been planning to enter into the competition for the new build, in order to open the topmost desk drawer. After rummaging around for a while, he found the worn-out looking notebook that he had once used to record important phone numbers. He hoped the number hadn't changed. After all, it was over fifteen years since he last dialled it.

It rang for what felt like an eternity, before someone picked up.

'Dr Volwarth?'

'Speaking. Who is this?'

'It's me. Leon Nader. I think it's started again.'

# 4

'Thank you for coming so quickly.'

Dr Samuel Volwarth acknowledged Leon's conversation opener with an indulgent smile and made himself comfortable on the sofa. 'I don't normally do house calls, but I have to admit, you made me curious. Yet again.'

Leon had reached the psychiatrist just as he was about to set off on a trip. Dr Volwarth was due to depart for a congress in Tokyo and had made a detour on his way to the airport to pay a flying visit to his former patient.

Now they were sat in the living room while the taxi outside waited on double yellow lines. But despite this, Volwarth looked completely relaxed and composed, just as Leon remembered him. It was a peculiar feeling to be sitting opposite him again, after such a long time.

The psychiatrist didn't look to have aged by even a day. As before, his hair was long and tied in a grey ponytail. It seemed he was still making the greatest effort to be different. But his appearance, despite being scandalous to Leon back in his childhood, now just looked extrovert: Volwarth's leather trousers, his cowboy boots, the swallow tattoo on his neck. Searching for signs of the passing of time, Leon could only find them in the details: the corners of his mouth drooping a little lower, the rings under his eyes a shade darker. And the doctor had replaced his pearl earring with a discreet silver stud.

'It's been a hell of a long time, hasn't it? Almost an entire beach must have passed through the hourglass since we last saw each other.'

Leon nodded. It was seventeen years since his concerned parents had driven him to Volwarth's private clinic for the first time.

Back then, however, he still hadn't called Klaus and Maria his *parents*. In the first years after the accident, it would have felt like a betrayal of his biological parents, who he'd lost at the age of ten. A depressed, suicidal alcoholic had intentionally driven down the wrong slip road of the motorway. The head-on collision claimed three victims. Only two passengers survived: Leon, who even now could remember that he and his sister were singing along to 'Yellow Submarine' on the radio when the headlights suddenly appeared ahead of them; and the wrong-way driver, who came out of it with just a broken collarbone. An ironic twist of fate that only the Devil could find amusing.

The days after Leon had woken up in hospital as an orphan felt like living under a diving bell. He listened to the doctors' diagnoses, the recommendations of the child psychologists and the words of the woman from the youth welfare office, but he didn't understand them. The lips of those who examined him, cared for him and – in the end – wanted to offload him to replacement parents, had moved and produced noise but no meaning.

'It's a lovely place you have here,' said the psychiatrist now, almost two decades later, his gaze fixed on the stuccoed ceiling. 'An old build with a lift and parquet floor. South-facing balcony, and I guess around four bedrooms. It can't have been easy to find something like that in this neighbourhood.'

'Three bedrooms. But yes, it was definitely the proverbial needle in the haystack.'

Natalie had stumbled across the rental notice by chance while out for a walk and had written to the owner without holding out any great hopes. They even thought it might be a hoax, because a choice piece of property like this was more likely to be advertised in the glossy catalogues of the luxury estate agents than on the post of a street lamp.

They'd spent a whole year on the waiting list and had to submit one guarantee after another before finally being accepted by the building management. Even today Leon still didn't know what tipped the balance in their favour, making them come out ahead of a host of other applicants. Such a desirable and far-from-cheap apartment would normally only be granted to tenants with a fixed income. Not to two freelancers with uncertain commission prospects.

'Did you know that I recently spoke about your case again at a symposium?' the psychiatrist suddenly asked.

Volwarth seemed to be observing Leon's every reaction, and – not for the first time since the doctor walked into the apartment – Leon felt like he was back in the therapy sessions that had defined a significant part of his childhood. While other boys were heading out to the Baggersee, playing football in the gravel pit or making a treehouse in the garden, this man had been cabling him up, plugging him into a computer and rummaging around in his soul with his never-ending questions.

'So what was the catalyst that made you want to see me?'

Leon stood up. 'That's what I'd like to show you.'

He turned the television on with the remote control. The ancient video recorder underneath, however, he had to operate manually. He had hauled it up from the cellar just an hour before, given it a quick dust and connected it to the flatscreen monitor. It was a miracle the clunky monstrosity still worked. The spooling VHS tape crackled with every turn like a badly oiled cog.

'You kept our old tapes?' asked Volwarth in astonishment as he saw the first images appear on the screen. He had given them to Leon at their last session, as a parting gift from the successfully completed therapy.

'Well, would you look at that.'

Volwarth had stood up right next to Leon, his gaze fixed on the screen.

The grainy, slightly yellowed images showed Leon's eleven-year-old face in close-up. Back then he had still been chubby-cheeked and a little dumpy, not anywhere near as slim as he was today. On the recording, he was sat bolt upright in his pyjamas on the edge of a bed in a child's room. The bed-sheets were those of a popular football team, and a poster of Michael Jackson had been tacked on to the wardrobe in the background. He hadn't chosen either of them. Nor the bed, the room or the adoptive parents into whose care he had been passed. They were already the second couple to try with him. But they were the first to enlist a doctor to get to the bottom of his problems.

'Do you know what we're planning to do tonight, Leon?' asked Volwarth on the tape. Even his voice sounded just the same as it did today. The psychiatrist was standing out of sight behind the camera, into which little Leon was blinking nervously. His eyes were red-rimmed and he looked exhausted, because he had slept only a few minutes for the third night in a row. But he nodded.

'It's an experiment that we haven't yet carried out with a child of your age. It's completely harmless, nothing will happen to you. I just want you to know this: nothing will happen against your will here. You can tell me if you'd prefer not to do it after all.'

'No, it's OK. But it won't hurt, will it?'

'No,' laughed Dr Volwarth good-naturedly. 'It might pinch a little when you lie down, but we've cushioned everything well.'

With these words, the psychiatrist appeared in the picture. His back obscured the view for a brief moment, then Volwarth could be seen trying to fasten something to the boy's head. When he stepped aside again, Leon was wearing a shining metal ring that ran around his forehead, with a fist-sized object attached to it that was vaguely reminiscent of a miner's lamp.

'The thing on your head is a radio-controlled sleep camera,' explained Volwarth in a calm voice.

'And it films everything I do while I'm dreaming?'

'Yes, it's motion-activated, which means it comes on as soon as you get up. We've made an exception this time and left off the electrodes that measure your brainwaves and muscle and eye movement. There are no cables, so you can move around freely. There's just one thing I want you to do for me.'

'What?'

'This is the only device like this we have in the institute, and it was very expensive. So please don't take a shower with it on.'

Leon smiled, but his eyes looked sad. 'I don't know what I do when I'm asleep, though. I can never remember.'

'That's exactly why you're going to wear this sleep camera tonight.'

'And what if I do something bad again?'

Volwarth frowned. 'What do you mean *again*? We've spoken about this at length, Leon. You're a sleepwalker. There are thousands of sleepwalkers in this country alone, it's nothing bad.'

'So then why did the Molls want me to leave?'

Watching it now, years after he had said these words for

the first time, Leon winced. His stomach started to cramp up. *Moll.*

Too many unbidden memories were linked with this name. Today he knew that it hadn't been his first foster parents' fault. Leon understood why they wanted to be rid of him, even if, at the time, he felt like an unwanted pet brought back to the animal home for not being house-trained.

'Frau Moll thought I was a murderer. She screamed it in my face.'

'Because your foster mother was scared. You know yourself what she saw. It would have scared the heck out of you too, right?'

'I guess so.'

'You see, it's just a completely normal reaction. When someone sleepwalks, to others they look like a ghost. But it's not dangerous.'

'So why did I have a knife in my hand?'

*As I stood there in the children's bedroom. Over her son's bed.*

To this day it still wasn't clear if he really wanted to hurt nine-year-old Adrian that night. How Leon got into his bedroom was a complete mystery, because to get there he had to go down one floor, and the designer stairs in the Molls' house didn't have a banister, which made them a challenge even awake. But the biggest puzzle was the bread knife Adrian's mother caught the sleepwalking Leon with. He had been holding it in both hands, like a dagger, above the chest of the sleeping child. The knife wasn't from the Molls' kitchen, and Leon hadn't been able to explain how it came into his possession. This put as much fear into him as the question of what would have happened if Frau Moll hadn't been woken by the creaking floorboards and gone to check what was happening. Adrian himself had been completely unaware of both the sleeping visitor and the impending danger.

'Believe me, Leon. You're not a bad person,' Volwarth was saying on the tape. In spite of the bad picture quality, Leon could see in his own eyes that he didn't believe the doctor. Which was hardly a surprise.

The very next morning the Molls had informed the welfare office that they could no longer have him in their house. After a few days in the home he found a new place to stay with the Naders: a sweet-natured, childless couple who wanted a child much too desperately to be scared off by Leon's history. They did the right thing and obtained the best possible psychiatric treatment for him with Dr Volwarth, even though they couldn't really afford the expensive examinations, like the video analysis that Leon had dug out again now.

'With the help of that camera on your head, we'll be able to prove that there's a harmless explanation for everything,' said the young Dr Volwarth on the tape.

'Even for this?' The eleven-year-old leaned over and pulled a plastic bag out from under the bed, holding it up to the camera.

'Oh God,' exclaimed Volwarth as the child pulled an indefinable clump out of the bag and presented it to the camera.

'What the hell is that?'

# 5

Without waiting to hear the answer he had given the doctor back then, Leon stopped the video and gestured for Dr Volwarth to sit on the sofa.

'It's like it was yesterday,' said the psychiatrist with a far-away smile as he sank back down into the leather upholstery.

For him the images from the past seemed to wake pleasant memories, which was certainly not the case for Leon.

'You gave me a real shock back then, Leon. For a second I was genuinely scared that you were about to show me a dead animal.'

'No,' said Leon, reaching under the coffee table for the shoebox he had put there. He opened the lid and showed his guest the contents. 'Luckily, it wasn't an animal.'

'You kept *these* too?' asked Volwarth.

Leon shook his head. 'They're not the same trainers. I found them in my microwave this morning.'

'Today?'

Volwarth leaned over, looking intrigued.

'Yes. This morning. The day after my wife left me.'

The psychiatrist reached for the stud in his earlobe and played with it for a moment.

'You're married,' he asked after a brief pause.

The question surprised Leon.

'Yes. Why?'

'You're not wearing a ring,' explained Volwarth.

'Sorry?'

Leon touched the ring finger on his left hand (Natalie had suggested they wore them on the side of their hearts, even though in Germany it was traditional to wear them on the right) and, confused, registered only the indent in his skin left behind by the ring.

'I must have taken it off in the bathroom,' he murmured, even though that was practically impossible. It was much too tight and could barely be moved even with oil or soap. Leon had been planning to take it to the jeweller's.

Volwarth fixed him with a long analytical stare, then asked: 'Do you want to have children?'

'Yes, definitely. Natalie stopped taking the pill the day we moved in here, about a year ago now.'

'But she left you anyway?'

'It looks that way.'

Leon summarised the peculiar events for Dr Volwarth, who became increasingly agitated as the story progressed, before clapping his hands together and cutting Leon off: 'No matter what you say, I don't believe you did anything to your wife in your sleep.'

'But we can't rule it out.'

Volwarth made an appeasing hand gesture and clicked his tongue. 'Theoretically, sure. In the decades that I've been researching and treating parasomnias, I've encountered almost everything: people who clean their apartments in the deep-sleep phase, sleepwalkers who have coherent conversations with their partners and even answer questions. I had patients who did washing in the night and even operated complicated devices. In one case a marketing manager typed entire presentations into his computer and sent them by email to his co-workers. Another got into the car while asleep and drove twenty-three kilometres to the neighbouring town . . .'

'. . . to stab his mother-in-law with a kitchen knife,' continued Leon.

Volwarth grimaced regretfully. 'Unfortunately, yes. The Kenneth Parks case was all over the press, and it wasn't the invention of some horror film director.'

'So there are people who become violent in their sleep,' persisted Leon.

'Yes, but that applies to less than one in a thousand sleepwalkers.'

'And what makes you so sure I'm not one of them?'

Volwarth's expression turned thoughtful, nodding as though Leon was a student who had asked a clever question.

'My experience tells me. And the results of my studies. As you know, somnambulism is one of the least-researched phenomena in medicine. But in recent years my clinic has made some ground-breaking discoveries. Starting with the fact that the very definition "sleepwalking" is flawed. Sure, the night-time activities mostly occur in the deep-sleep phase, but strictly speaking the so-called sleepwalker isn't actually asleep. He is in another, barely researched stage of consciousness between being asleep and awake. I call it the third stage.'

Leon tugged nervously at the skin over his Adam's apple. Volwarth's descriptions reminded him of his own sleep paralysis, from which he always struggled to wake.

'In long-term studies, where we put the entire family under clinical observation, we were able to find out that the sleepwalkers' violence is primarily directed towards loved ones.'

'There you go!' Leon clapped his hands together. 'Now you yourself are saying that—'

'But . . .' Volwarth raised his index finger '. . . there are always warning signs. Had Natalie ever complained that you were rough with her in your sleep?'

'No.'

'Did you ever strangle or hit her in the night?'

'I don't know.'

'Believe me, you would know if you had. Of course you can't remember your night-time activity the next morning, but your wife would certainly have told you. Sleepwalkers don't just tear their partners' fingernails out from one night to the next, or punch their teeth in. It begins gradually.'

'But I saw it,' retorted Leon.

'What exactly did you see?'

'Her bruised eye,' answered Leon with agitation. 'I already told you about Natalie's injuries.'

'But you also told me that you had just woken up from a horrible nightmare involving a cockroach.'

'What's your point?' asked Leon, feeling rattled.

The psychiatrist leaned forwards on the sofa. 'It was dark. Could it perhaps have just been eye make-up, which in your half-asleep state you confused with a black eye?'

'I don't think so, no. And that wouldn't explain her thumb-nail, either.'

*Or the broken tooth.*

'And she was limping.'

'Your wife was carrying a heavy suitcase. Even I was limping earlier when I had to haul mine to the taxi.'

'So how do you explain this?'

Leon waved the warped shoes around, like a piece of evidence in a courtroom. This was exactly how the pair looked that he had put in the oven at his foster parents' house while sleepwalking, just a few days after he arrived there.

A teasing smile danced on the doctor's lips. His gaze wandered to the empty wine bottle on the sideboard.

'Were you drinking alone?'

'Yes, but—'

'The whole bottle?'

Leon sighed, irritated at himself for not having cleared it away. 'My wife was late coming home. I opened the bottle anyway and I guess I lost track of how much I was drinking.'

'And you can't remember what happened after that, right? You don't know how you got undressed and into bed. You didn't notice when Natalie came home. And maybe you also forgot what you did to your trainers?'

Leon shook his head. 'Why would I nuke my trainers in the microwave while I was drunk?'

'Well, why would you hit your wife?'

Dr Volwarth looked at the clock and repeated what he had said in the video recording: 'I'm sure there's a harmless explanation for all of this. It's possible that Natalie came home late, got mad because you were drunk, and went to stay with her best friend for a few days.'

'I already called her.'

'Well, maybe she's gone to a hotel. The problems in your relationship didn't appear overnight, am I correct?'

Leon nodded absent-mindedly.

'Is it because of the miscarriage?'

The question hit Leon like a slap in the face.

'How do you know about that?' he asked, stunned.

'It was a shot in the dark. You told me you've been trying for a baby for almost a year now. But I don't see any baby books, or catalogues for changing tables and prams on the coffee table, not even the slightest sign of nesting.'

Leon nodded pensively, feeling strangely exposed.

When they managed to secure their dream apartment,

they saw it as a good omen for the future. But things had changed after the miscarriage.

'And how are things going professionally?' was Dr Volwarth's next question.

'Natalie just opened a gallery with her best friend,' answered Leon, happy to change the subject.

'I meant with you.'

'Oh, right. Everything's great there too, technically.'

'And non-technically?'

'We're in the middle of a bid for a big project. Sven and I—'

'Who is Sven?'

'Sven Berger, my best friend and co-owner of the practice. He was the one who pulled in this big potential commission. A children's hospital. Our first designs went down really well, and we have a good chance of winning the commission. I just need to make a few changes and submit the scale model by Thursday at the latest.'

Volwarth looked at the time again. 'That's in a few days' time. So you're not just under extreme stress personally, but professionally too.' He stood up.

'Yes. I mean . . . no. That's not the problem.' Leon, who had stood now too, knew what the psychiatrist was getting at. He had suffered from sleep disturbances even before the car accident, but they had got worse afterwards. It was only when he found a caring home with the Naders that the emotional pressure started to recede. His subconscious had finally been able to find some peace. The stronger the love for his foster parents became, the less reason he had to run from his fears in the night. That was Volwarth's theory, who back then had seemed almost sad that Leon's violent outburst at the Molls had not repeated itself. The trainers had been the last act of destruction, and they hadn't even been living things.

'How can you be so sure?' Leon persisted as they walked out of the living room. 'I mean, my behaviour was strange even as a child.'

'Strange, but not violent, Leon. Countless sessions, dozens of recordings, and we weren't able to document a single violent attack.'

'Maybe there's nothing on the tapes because we stopped the experiment too soon.'

Volwarth shook his head and, in a familiar gesture, laid his hand on Leon's shoulder. 'We didn't see anything because there was nothing to see; we knew that even before we put the sleep camera on your head.'

'Oh really? So why did you do it?'

'Because I didn't want to cure your somnambulism, but your psychosis. That's what made your case so interesting: you convinced yourself you were going to do something evil in your sleep. You were so scared that in the end you didn't want to go to sleep. And this fear of going to sleep, also known as hypnophobia, was what I wanted to take away from you with those tapes. Recordings that, when all is said and done, proved the only person you're a danger to is yourself, like if you bump into the corner of a table in your sleep or stumble over something. If anything, you probably would have injured yourself with that knife.'

He scrutinised Leon's face as though searching for a sign that he had got through. Then he sighed. 'To me it sounds like you're going through an emotional endurance test right now. And just like all those years ago, when everything got back on the right track after you were taken in by the right people, things will figure themselves out once the stress has abated a little.'

Leon wanted to interject, but Volwarth didn't give him the opportunity.

'I have a suggestion for you: complete your work for the

bid, submit the model, give your wife a few days of space, and once things have calmed down a bit, come into my lab and we'll plug you in again and have a more detailed look if that would put your mind at rest. OK?'

Volwarth took a prescription pad from the back pocket of his leather trousers and asked to borrow a pen. Leon moved to hand him his fountain pen from the telephone table, but it wasn't there, even though he was sure he'd seen it just recently.

'No problem.' Volwarth pulled a biro from his jacket pocket, scribbled a few indecipherable words, then tore off the slip of paper and handed it to Leon.

'What's this?'

'A gentle sedative. It's based on a herbal remedy and helps to provide a dreamless sleep. The dose I've prescribed should last you until I'm back in the country again.'

'Nocturnalon,' Leon read out loud.

Once the psychiatrist was gone, Leon suddenly felt so tired it was as though he'd already taken a whole packet of it.

# 6

'Do it!'

The sex was like it always was. Wild, unrestrained and of an intensity that would be embarrassing to him as soon as he could think straight again. But right now orgasm was still a myriad of kicks, bites and screams of lust away. Right now Leon was still relishing whispering all the frivolous abuse into Natalie's ear that he knew turned her on so much.

*Bitch. Slut.*

Normally she just repeated the insults. As if she had earned them.

*Because I've been a naughty girl.*

But today she threw him off his rhythm with an unexpected request.

'Come on, do it!'

Leon grabbed at her breasts, pulling her closer.

'No, not like that.'

He slowed down.

'How?'

She reached for his hand and pulled it to her face.

'Hit me,' she gasped beneath him.

Leon propped himself up with his hands either side of her head, in confusion.

'Do it. Please.'

Natalie grabbed his ass and pulled him deeper inside her.
*Hit you?*

'I don't understand. How—'

'What is there not to understand?' It was another voice. He looked to the right and froze in shock as he recognised his mother sitting on the chair next to the bed. 'The horny slut wants it harder.' She grinned wantonly. 'It's not like you have to reach straight for the whip like your father. A slap will do for now.'

Leon felt his penis go limp inside Natalie.

*What's going on?*

'It'll figure itself out. It does in most cases.'

The words were coming from his wife's mouth, but Natalie was suddenly speaking with the grating voice of an old man. It took a while before Leon recognised the officer he had spoken to after saying goodbye to Dr Volwarth yesterday, when he had called the police station to file a missing person's report.

'With adults we don't tend to start looking into it until fourteen days after the disappearance.'

Leon's mother, too, was now speaking in the voice of the detective as she said: 'Just wait for a while, then give the whore a good hiding if she turns up.'

*No!* Leon wanted to scream, but he couldn't utter a single sound.

He tried to disentangle himself from Natalie, but the more he tried, the weaker he became. She reached for his hand and pressed his fingers into a fist. He tried to wriggle free, but couldn't, it was as though his joints had been locked. Leon felt Natalie grab him by the wrist, spurred on by the cheers of encouragement from his mother. Then she smiled and opened her mouth, inside which a living thing was moving around.

*Morphet!*

The cockroach's feelers came darting out from between

her lips like the tongue of a snake. And Natalie rammed Leon's fist into her face.

There was a crunching sound, as though he had kicked in a rotten old door. At the same time he heard a dull echo.

'Bull's-eye,' laughed Natalie, spitting out a piece of her front tooth. As she did so, Morphet crawled from her mouth and scuttled across her cheek towards her eye.

*Oh God,* screamed Leon silently, unable to stop it from happening. Powerless to stop her, he let Natalie use his own fist to beat herself with again. This time on her open eye, where the cockroach had positioned itself, its pincers about to bore into her pupil.

'Hit me. I deserve it.'

Natalie magnified the force of the punches by jerking her head forward just before impact. There was a popping sound like an exploding air balloon as Leon's fist crushed her eyeball.

Then another sound was reverberating in his head, high and sonorous. Leon sat up in shock. He blindly fumbled around for the cordless telephone on his nightstand, surprised that it wasn't on the unit in the hallway where he normally put it before going to bed so that the ancient thing could charge overnight. Part of his consciousness was still imprisoned in the nightmare, but the other part registered the familiar number on the vibrating display.

'Where the hell are you?' said Sven. 'We were supposed to go through the presentation!'

His best friend was really mad, that was clear from the tiny pauses scattered between his words.

When he was younger Sven's stutter had been much more pronounced, and Leon was the only one in their class who hadn't bullied him for it. Their deep bond of friendship, much more than a mere working relationship, was based primarily on a foundation of respect that had been obvious even at

46

the tender age of fourteen. Leon accepted Sven's speech impediment, and Sven didn't see him as an exotic orphan like many of their other classmates did. To this day Sven believed that it was thanks to Leon's friendship and the increased confidence it gave him that he was finally able to overcome the stuttering. Nowadays it was only noticeable to those who knew him, and then only when he was very worked up. Leon, however, felt certain that it was much more down to the speech therapist whose exercises Sven still followed even now.

'I, I . . . oh damn.' Leon looked at the alarm clock on his nightstand; the thing must have stopped, because it was showing 4 a.m., and Sven would never call him in the middle of the night.

'Shit.'

'Yes, exactly. I've been waiting for you in the office for an hour now. Where are you?'

'Sorry, I overslept.'

'Overslept?' asked Sven in disbelief. 'We were planning to go through the alterations. It's gone six in the evening!'

'What?'

That was impossible. Leon had gone to bed very early last night because of a persistent headache making it impossible for him to carry on working. He didn't take one of the sleeping tablets that Volwarth had prescribed. He didn't even leave the house to pick up the prescription, and it was impossible that he could have slept that long. Although the headache had subsided, he still felt numb and woozy.

'I think I must be coming down with something,' he mumbled into the receiver.

'Don't get sick on me, Leon. Don't slack off when we're on the home stretch.'

'I won't, don't worry. The model will be ready.'

'Man, this thing with Natalie really seems to have thrown you for a loop.'

47

'Natalie?'

Leon sat up straight in shock.

*How does he know about that?*

'Yes. Has she turned up yet?'

'No,' said Leon in confusion.

He pushed the bed-sheet off and noticed to his surprise that he was only wearing boxer shorts. He was sure he remembered having fallen into bed fully clothed, exhausted.

*Did I get drunk again? For God's sake, what else can't I remember?*

A ringing sound, similar to the one in the dream, made Leon jump. He stood up.

'Hang on, I have to answer the front door.'

He padded barefoot into the hallway. Before he opened the door, he looked through the peephole. Relief flooded through him.

*Thank God.*

At least his memory hadn't let him down with this. He had spent ages searching on the internet yesterday before finally finding what he was looking for, and, as promised, the company was delivering the very next day.

'Just a moment,' called Leon through the closed door. He grabbed a coat from the cloakroom before opening the door to the delivery guy.

The man, who was around Leon's age, wore a uniform that was threadbare at the knees and elbows, the brown of which matched his closely shorn hair. The name badge above the company logo (*United Deliveries – We Love What We Do*) declared him to be Jonas K., although Jonas K. didn't appear to identify with the logo particularly. He was chewing gum listlessly and listening to music on clunky headphones.

While Leon awkwardly scribbled his signature on a clipboard, he promised Sven he would bring the new designs into the office that evening. 'I've arranged the lifts around the atrium to save space. And there's a show-stopper that the clinic management are going to love.'

He was just about to close the door when the courier took off his headphones abruptly and said, 'Excuse me, I have a problem.'

'Sorry?'

'Could I use your toilet quickly?'

'What?'

'Your toilet. You do have one, don't you?'

Leon blinked nervously; the question was too much for him right now. A reasonable request that was just as difficult to grant as it was to refuse.

He took a closer look at the man. Now that he had stopped chewing gum, he looked a lot more intelligent. A high forehead, alert eyes, his nose a little too big in relation to the rest, albeit not damaging the overall impression any more than the missing left earlobe, which only became noticeable now he'd taken off the headphones.

Leon stepped to the side to let the uninvited guest pass.

'Thank you, that's very kind. I have diarrhoea, you see.'

'Excuse me?'

Leon thought he must have misheard, but the man's expression didn't change. It was only after a few moments that his trembling lower lip betrayed him. 'Oh man, you should take a look at your face in the mirror,' he choked, exploding with laughter. 'You look as though you just shit your own pants.'

Now the courier was laughing manically at his own absurd joke, while Leon struggled to bring his expression back under control.

*Has everyone here gone crazy?*

'No harm meant, mate, but I have to keep my spirits up with this tedious job somehow.' With a chuckle, the joker put his headphones back on and turned on his heel.

'Who was that?' asked Sven, once Leon had closed the door.

'Just some weirdo. Where was I?'

He looked through the peephole, but the courier had disappeared.

'You were telling me about the show-stopper you've built into the presentation.'

'So I was. An underground tunnel system, connecting the most important wings of the hospital. But not just for pedestrians, as is usually the case: for emergency vehicles too.'

'Which means we've solved the radiology problem and patient transport,' said Sven with delight. Their first designs had been criticised for the location of the diagnosis centre – it was too out of the way. An inevitable problem arising from the rambling hospital grounds. 'And we can keep the basic concept.'

'Yes. Let's just hope they accept the enormous additional costs.'

With the telephone clamped between his chin and collarbone, Leon carried the package in both hands along the hallway to his study, pushing the door open with his foot.

'As I already said, I like it a lot,' said Sven. 'But we still need to discuss it in detail. You're coming to the party with me, right?'

'Yes, of course,' answered Leon tonelessly, not paying attention. His feeling of elation at Sven's approval had evaporated the second he walked into the study.

With his gaze fixed on the empty desk, he said softly, 'But please give me a bit more time.'

*What the hell is happening here?*

The scale model, the one he had been working on day and night for the last few weeks, was no longer where he had left it.

# 7

'Natalie? Please just call me back, will you? I'm out of my mind with worry.'

With the telephone to his ear, Leon flung open one door after another: bedroom, hallway, kitchen, lounge-diner. A fleeting glance was enough. For an object the size of a suitcase, there were very few possible hiding places even in their large apartment, and Leon was unable to find it in any of them. The model had completely vanished.

Leon couldn't make sense of it. The cardboard model had been on the desk, there and nowhere else. Besides that, it was much too bulky to move around. He had been dreading carrying the cumbersome thing into the office by himself. If he had sleepwalked with it, he wouldn't have had a free hand to close the door behind him afterwards.

*But it was ajar*, he thought, ending his one-sided conversation with Natalie's voicemail. As with the previous attempts to call her, the voicemail had kicked in after ten rings.

He went into the bathroom and pushed the shower curtain aside, but of course he didn't find the model of the hospital there, nor on the balcony overlooking the courtyard or on top of the wardrobe. He even looked outside the front door. By now he was doubting his sanity so much that he checked every room a second time, starting with Natalie's most holy place: her dark room.

The windowless, tiled room at the far end of the T-shaped hallway had originally been intended as a guest bathroom; now it housed a small laboratory bench and ventilation system, several fixed sinks and a lockable chemicals cupboard next to the washbasin. Natalie had created an additional partition behind the door, using a light-excluding theatre curtain, beyond which Leon had ventured three times at most since they moved in. The dark room was Natalie's territory, a foreign land for which he had no entry visa.

Again, he felt like an intruder, like he was doing something wrong.

He pressed the switch next to the partition, and the red lamp bathed the room in hazy light.

Hidden away somewhere, so that it couldn't be turned on by accident, was the switch for the conventional ceiling light. But Leon wasn't in the mood to search for it, and the lamp gave enough light anyway.

Nothing stood out, apart from a disturbing black-and-white photograph that Natalie had clipped to a washing line. The picture showed her face on a stranger's torso – that of a naked, pregnant woman. It was obviously a montage, but a very good one, because it was impossible to make out a single flaw in the transition from neck to chest.

Natalie must have created the image for the exhibition that Anouka was now working on alone.

*Star Children.*

Leon looked around more carefully this time, noticing prints of other, slightly modified motifs of the pregnant woman, still swimming in the fixing baths.

He took a step closer.

The smell of the developer was almost impossible to bear, but he didn't know how to turn on the ventilation system.

Leon's eyes filled with tears. One of the pictures floating under the red light, as though in a pool of blood, became more blurred every time he blinked.

*That's impossible.*

Leon wanted to turn away, but the pornographic brutality of the image had an almost magnetic allure. He leaned forward, feeling his stomach flip like he was on a roller-coaster just before it plunged into the abyss for the first time.

*This can't be real.*

It wasn't so much the manipulated image that shocked him, which was of Natalie, her eyes closed, ramming a broken bottle neck into her rounded belly; it was the object swimming in the fixing bath: a string of artificial pearls. And there was no doubt who it belonged to.

Natalie's name was on the pink identity bracelet, the good-luck charm, the one that had been swinging from her mobile phone as she ran from the apartment.

# 8

When asked how they met, Leon and Natalie tended to keep quiet and just smile. Sometimes they told the truth, joining in with the questioner's laughter as though to confirm they were joking. But they really had met for the first time in a brothel, and it had been La Fola, one of the most renowned in the city.

At the time neither of them believed the other's explanation as to what had brought them there. He had been on a stag night, while she was looking for inspiration for her final project at art college, entitled 'The Naked Society'.

The music was as loud as in a nightclub, meaning that Leon had to lean in close to Natalie to read her words from her lips. They were marked by the gentle impressions of her front teeth and a little torn at the corners of her mouth, but that didn't stop her from grinning broadly at much of his conversation. Even the parts that weren't funny in the slightest.

'I hate photos,' he had admitted to her hours later, after he had parted company with his friends. They had gone for a walk together, without giving so much as a glance at the window displays of the over-expensive boutiques along the boulevard. 'Especially photos of myself. I'm not very photogenic.'

As proof, he presented his ID photo.

'The photographer obviously didn't like you,' she said, and even though he laughed at the observation, Leon knew she hadn't meant it as a joke.

Natalie opened her handbag and pulled out a Polaroid camera.

Before he could protest, she had pressed the button. While waving the print around like a fan, she explained her theory to him: 'The greater the love of the photographer for their subject, the better the picture.'

Leon stared speechless at the photograph in his hands.

'And do you like yourself?' she asked.

'Much more than in real life,' he admitted, feeling a bit dazed.

A little later they kissed.


*How can something that began so perfectly end so terribly?* thought Leon as he sat there in his study, only a few weeks after their third anniversary, opening the package that had just arrived.

At first glance the order seemed complete: an elastic head-band, two motion sensors, Velcro tape, cable, batteries, a USB stick.

*And of course the radio-controlled camera.*

Admittedly it didn't look exactly the same as the model he had picked online, but it wasn't the first time the shop had delivered the wrong thing. And in this case it was to Leon's advantage, for the camera had a higher resolution than the one he had actually ordered.

He carried everything into the bedroom, where he had already started up the laptop on the bureau. A hypnophobia forum online had ended up being a real treasure trove of information. Leon was clearly not the only person wanting to film himself in his sleep.

As he fastened the camera to the headband with the Velcro tape, he felt himself starting to get sleepy. *But I already slept for an eternity, damn it. What's wrong with me?*

His desire to sleep increased with the speed of the progress bar on the screen as the camera's software installed on the computer.

He then had to carry out a function test by lying motion-less on the bed, which was astonishingly difficult despite his tiredness. His nerves were jangling. After just a minute he sat back up again to check whether the motion sensors had sent a radio impulse to the component in the USB slot of the laptop, activating the filming function.

*Bingo.*

The green LED lamp of the USB stick blinked in rhythm with his heartbeat, showing Leon the recording status. When he took the headband off again and laid it next to him on the pillow, the colour changed from green to red. The recording stopped as soon as the camera went into standby mode.

Leon stood up and went over to the bureau. Moving the mouse nervously, he opened the video player's display window. The brief recording was just one megabyte in size and started immediately as he clicked.

Leon stared at what his head movements had managed to capture, overcome by a confusing sensation, similar to the one he'd had when he heard a recording of his voice for the first time. He saw his bed-sheets, followed the camera panning over the wardrobe to the monitor, which was flick-ering feverishly on the recording, and felt like a stranger in his home.

So as not to be woken by the sun rising, he lowered the blinds and pulled the curtains. The camera had an infrared recording function and a low-light amplifier that was consid-erably more sensitive than the bulky thing Dr Volwarth had attached to him all those years ago.

Despite the jeans and thick sweatshirt he had on, he was cold with fatigue, and contemplated taking a bath to help him sleep. But he was afraid nothing would stop the thoughts exploding in his mind. Eventually, he drank a glass of red wine and pulled on a thick pair of socks with soles of rubberised dots. Then he put on the headband with the camera, laid down in bed, and waited for his eyes to close.

# 9

Leon had always been the kind of person who brooded over things. While Natalie could simply turn over and fall asleep even after a heated argument, he would often lie awake for hours on end, staring at the ceiling and trying to get to the bottom of things.

He could still remember clearly the last time he found himself in a similar, almost schizophrenic state of limbo, in which his body was screaming for sleep but his mind for answers. It had been after that unfortunate dinner when he met Natalie's parents for the first time.

Leon had arrived alone in the expensive Italian restaurant, where the walls looked like the event pages of a society magazine: every centimetre adorned with pictures of politicians, singers, actors, artists. All of them grinning broadly, arm in arm with the owner as though he were their best friend and not just a clever businessman primarily interested in gratifying his own vanity.

Leon felt uncomfortable from the start. Not because of the ambience, but because he was a coward who had disowned his own parents. Unlike Hector, Natalie's father, Klaus Nader couldn't afford Savile Row suits, not on his waiter's salary. He would choose wine not by taste but by price, if at all. And if presented with a wine list dominated by expensive bottles, his likely response would be to ask for a menu where the prices weren't given in Turkish lira.

And what would they have talked about? Certainly not about whether it was better to winter in Florida or Mauritius to flee the awful weather. Maria Nader was just happy if the tram tracks didn't freeze up in January, and she was more likely to worry about whether the special offer from the newspaper supplement would still be available the next day than whether seat 4C in first class with Emirates was the best around. His adoptive parents, who had adopted him shortly before his sixteenth birthday, had travelled first class just once. And that had been by train, and only because they got into the wrong carriage by mistake.

Yet the evening didn't get off to the stilted beginning Leon had feared. Hector and Silvia Lené might look like they had just jumped out of the pages of a brochure for luxury retirement properties – healthy, dripping with jewellery, suntanned and full of energy, albeit still unmistakably in the autumn of their lives – but Hector relaxed the atmosphere with some humorous and witty anecdotes, which surprisingly weren't about financial investments or second homes, nor about his passion for collecting classic cars. He even complained about the steep prices in the restaurant, rolling his eyes at the small portions, and Leon became increasingly ashamed at having made a cheap excuse for his parents' absence. In all likelihood everyone would have got on well; he was probably the only snob at this table, one who had failed to stand by the people who loved him unconditionally. Even though the Naders didn't share Leon's interest in architecture and had never been to university, they had sacrificed a car, holidays and other comforts just to finance his studies.

He felt sick as he realised how badly he had acted, how great was his betrayal. Leon could try to convince himself that he just wanted to spare his parents the embarrassment of having to pick up the cheque (their pride would have prevented them from yielding to their son), but in truth he knew he was ashamed of his background and that this was why he'd made a cheap excuse as to why Mum and Dad were unfortunately feeling under the weather today.

He had decided to make up for his mistake and quickly suggest an invitation in return, when something happened to make it crystal clear there would be no further meeting. Not with his parents. Not with him. Never again.

It happened in the toilets. Leon was standing at the urinal when Hector walked in and positioned himself at the next basin, humming cheerfully. Leon was trying to hit the sticker of a fly attached to the urinal as a target, when Hector addressed him: 'She likes it dirty.'

'Excuse me?'

Hector winked at him and unzipped his fly. 'I know I shouldn't say that, as her father. But as men we can speak openly, right? You're not a prude or something, are you?'

'No, of course not,' said Leon, trying to force a smile. He glanced over only briefly, and his gaze inadvertently landed on the hand of his future father-in-law, whose member was either half erect or unusually large. The stream splattering down on to the enamel was correspondingly loud and intense.

'Good, I'm glad to hear it. Because I wouldn't marry my daughter off to some uptight faggot. She needs a proper stallion.'

'Sorry?'

'She gets it from her mother. You might not think it, to look at her now. But under the slap, Silvia's still the same exhibitionist hussy whose virginity I took over forty years ago.'

Leon's fake smile began to choke him. He was still hoping

60

that Hector would cry out 'I had you going there for a minute!' and clout him on the shoulder with his massive paw. But Natalie's father was deadly serious.

'Like mother, like daughter. It's no secret that Natalie was unbelievably horny even from an early age. And so blatant about it. She always left her bedroom door open when her boyfriends stayed the night. And there were more than a few!'

Hector laughed and shook himself off. 'I didn't want to see it, Leon. But Natalie made it impossible for me not to. That's how I know what she gets off on. Handcuffs, collars. Pulled really tight, like on a mangy dog.'

He pulled his zipper up, then, noticing Leon's amazement, gave him a questioning look.

'Hey, this stays between us, OK? I mean, we are family now, aren't we?'

'Of course,' Leon stuttered, and didn't say a word for the rest of the dinner. He felt even more ashamed than before; at the beginning of the meal he had genuinely regretted that his own father wasn't as worldly, well read or cultured as Hector. At the end he was furious he didn't give Hector a piece of his mind and take a swing for him when, as Hector said goodbye, he let his hand rest on Natalie's behind for a brief moment. And Leon hated himself because he knew he would never work up the courage to tell Natalie about the conversation in the men's room, because that would not only have poisoned her love for her father, but possibly her love for him too.

*And I can't risk that. I can't risk losing you*, thought Leon now, years later.

With the thought, the memory of that awful dinner began to fade.

He opened his eyes, and the nightmare was over.

# 10

When he sat up in bed, Leon didn't know where he was. Normally the light from the aquarium woke him. Today the darkness around him was so intense that he lost his sense of orientation.

For the first few seconds he thought he was imprisoned in another sleep paralysis and was dreaming his fruitless attempts to reach out for a light source. Wherever he stretched out his hand, he grasped into nothingness.

*Natalie, where are you?* was his first clear thought as he realised he was lying in bed alone.

*And why do the bed-sheets feel so strange?*

He traced his fingers over the cotton, missing the warm imprint of her body as she slept. Where was her familiar scent, that mix of fresh hay and green tea he could usually smell even hours after she had got up?

In that moment all he could smell was his own stale breath, and the sheet felt unusually smooth.

*And numb.*

Exactly. *Numb.* That was the right word.

Leon clawed his fingers into the sheet, made a fist, and as his eyes slowly became accustomed to the scant light in the bedroom, he remembered why he had woken alone.

And why, hovering a short distance away, a little red light was blinking.

With a start, he sat up and rubbed his eyes.

*The computer. The recording.*

Leon reached his hand up to his forehead, but the camera wasn't there.

*Was it just a dream after all? But if so, then why is the USB stick blinking?*

He rolled to the left, grappling around on the nightstand until he found the switch for his reading lamp. When he turned it on, he screamed out.

It was a brief, involuntary reflex that he would have been ashamed of in Natalie's company, but he couldn't remember ever having been so shocked in his life.

Not when, at the age of eleven, he was awoken by the screams of Adrian's mother as he stood there with the knife in his hand next to the child's bed. Nor when he first saw himself sleepwalk in Dr Volwarth's practice.

None of his therapy sessions had ever been as disturbing as this moment, as he looked at his own hands to find they were covered in pale-green latex gloves.

*What in God's name . . .?*

In the light of the reading lamp, he stared at his fingers like a lunatic realising in a rare moment of clarity that he had just committed a crime.

That's why the sheet felt numb!

*That's why my hands feel like they don't belong to my body.*

Repulsed, he tore off the surgical gloves and threw them next to the bed. The elastic had clung so tightly to his wrists that his fingertips were shrivelled as though he had spent too long in the bath.

He pushed back the bedcovers and crawled out of bed. He was even colder than he had been before going to sleep, and felt like he hadn't slept for even a second, but a glance at his clock on the nightstand revealed the truth: fourteen hours had passed.

*What happened in that time?*

On the way over to his laptop Leon stumbled upon the headband with the camera attached to it. It was lying on the floor next to the wardrobe, and he resisted his first impulse to pick it up and put it back on.

An alarming thought shot into his mind: *This is a crime scene, you can't touch anything.*

Look, but don't touch!

Leon brushed a few carelessly discarded items of clothing from the chair and sat down on the heavy metal stool in front of the bureau. He opened the laptop and was blinded by the light of the monitor. Squinting, he opened the software. His fingers felt uncomfortably dry on the keyboard – they were still covered with the remains of talcum powder from the gloves.

His right eyelid began to twitch, a reflex Leon was unable to control. He guided the cursor of the mouse towards the replay button, then, after a few seconds of hesitation, clicked on it.

An input field popped up, requesting the password Leon had set up yesterday. He entered four digits, and the recording began. At first all he saw was shadows, which made him feel a little calmer. Despite his exhaustion, his body had clearly gone through several dream and deep-sleep phases, tossing and turning so restlessly in bed that the motion-activated camera was triggered. In the images, which had that typical greyish-green and slightly grainy look of those produced by a night-vision camera, he was able to make out how he trampled the blanket to the foot of the bed then pulled it up again, and how he gripped the big pillow like a life jacket, only to push it away a few minutes later.

As the camera only recorded while he was moving, during the first two hours of sleep it hadn't even captured ten minutes, and Leon began to hope that his nocturnal activity would be equally unspectacular to the end of the video film – that is, until the timer in the lower right-hand corner of the picture came to the 127th minute.

It began harmlessly. Even though Leon had expected these images, they were still a shock.

Suddenly, with a jolt, the perspective changed. He had sat up in his sleep, and now he was looking around. Slowly, as though he was seeing the room for the first time and wanted to commit every detail of it to his memory, the camera wandered from left to right. If the images before were unclear and flickering, now it was as though the camera was mounted on a tripod.

*Like a robot*, thought Leon, remembering that steady, mechanical movements were typical of sleepwalkers. Most roamed around like lifeless shells pulled by an invisible cord, and Leon was sure that the sight of them often awoke comparisons with zombies and the undead. His own movements, too, seemed like they were being steered by some unknown hand.

He recoiled in shock at the sight of himself, blurred by the camera shadows, as he walked in profile past the wall mirror next to the door. With the camera on his head, his appearance was reminiscent of the awful photographs of apes in animal laboratories when their skulls were opened up to measure their brain activity. Except that, unlike those poor creatures, he was not jammed into a clamp, but able to move around freely, albeit unconsciously.

The monitor went dark for a moment, then, two steps later, he was on Natalie's side of the bed, as he could see from all the photographs about underground bunker worlds that lay on her nightstand.

Leon turned round and compared the image with how things looked now. The photographs were still in the same place, exactly as in the video.

*But the drawer is open!*

Just as he turned back to the monitor, Leon's right hand wandered into the camera's field of vision. Holding his breath, he watched himself open Natalie's drawer and take out a pair of latex gloves.

*Why in God's name did she have something like that in her nightstand?*

Leon leaned forwards and grabbed the monitor with both hands as though he wanted to shake it. If someone had rung the doorbell right then, he wouldn't have heard it. They would have needed to set off a firework right next to his ear to tear his attention from the screen.

He wasn't sure if his brain was consciously slowing down the sequence of images, or if he really was pulling the gloves on as slowly and deliberately as the recording showed.

Leon tried to change the volume. Then he realised that, in his agitated state the day before, he had completely forgotten to activate the microphone software. So he was hearing the creak and snap of the gloves only in his imagination. Besides that, the recording was completely silent. No footsteps, no breathing, no rustling as he shuffled his way across the bedroom.

*Where am I going?*

Keeping his gaze fixed on the monitor, Leon reached down to touch the slipper socks on his feet, giving a start when his touch dislodged some dried earth from the bobbled soles.

*Where have I been?*

Leon watched himself march slowly but purposefully towards the wardrobe from which Natalie had been pulling her clothes in tears that unforgettable morning. Instead of opening it, as Leon expected himself to do, he paused,

66

motionless, in front of it. For so long, in fact, that the recording stopped. But then the pictures jolted back, with a quick pan upwards to the bedroom ceiling, and Leon walked into the gap between the bureau and the wardrobe.

He watched as, with a force he would have never thought himself capable of even in his conscious state, he pushed the old wardrobe to the side in his sleep.

*But why?*

Leon stopped the recording and looked at the wardrobe to his left. It was the only piece of furniture they had inherited from the previous owner, because Natalie had thought it so beautiful – now it looked like a threatening monolith, exerting an air of danger.

He stood up from the chair, his knees trembling.

He couldn't even begin to imagine how he had moved this heavy monstrosity in the night. Leon knelt down and felt the scrape marks on the parquet floor. They were neither slight nor new. Completely the opposite: deep grooves had been cut into the wood like train tracks, as though the wardrobe had frequently been moved back and forth over a long period of time.

Leon stood up once more.

Like on the recording, he pressed both hands against the side of the wardrobe, took a deep breath and pushed against it with all his strength. At first it refused to budge even a millimetre, but on the second try it moved with astonishing ease.

On the first attempt, admittedly, Leon had given himself a splinter when his hands slipped, and he found himself regretting having taken off the gloves. In the end he didn't need much longer than he had on the video. The wardrobe creaked and groaned, and the parquet floor screeched in protest, but after a few sweat-inducing seconds he had pushed the thing about a metre and a half to the side.

*And what now?*

Panting, he took a step back – and clapped his hand in front of his mouth.

*That's not possible.*

In disbelief, Leon stared at the object on the wall he had just exposed.

*I must be hallucinating.*

But there was no doubt.

Where the wardrobe had been just moments ago was a door that he had never seen before in his life.

# 11

*Do you see that door, there in the wall?*
  *Only a ghost can hear its call.*
  Suddenly, the melody was back. The ditty from his childhood – one of many that Leon's biological father had dreamed
up to embellish the bedtime stories he invented – was buzzing
around in Leon's head like a fly trapped under a glass.
  *Behind the door lies a hiding place.*
  *But don't go through. Run far, far away.*
  Even though he had never been into the strong room of
a bank, Leon imagined the doors to be just like the one he
was currently stretching his hand out towards. It looked
like the secure door to a vault containing important documents, money or gold bars.
  *Ignore this warning and it won't be long before*
  *You lose yourself behind the door.*
  The metal-clad door was barely a metre-eighty high, almost
his own height, and looked much too heavy and bulky for
the doorframe it was riveted to. In place of a door handle
were two tilted twist locks that had to be turned in a clockwise direction.
  *He who crosses the threshold at night*
  *Can never go back, try as hard as he might.*
  In total confusion Leon placed the palm of his hand

against the mysterious door. He had expected to hear a humming in his head, to see blurry, shadowy pictures dancing in front of his eyes, to perceive colours with more intensity or at least to smell some disturbing scent – something that would signal he was starting to lose his mind. But it seemed he wasn't yet teetering on the threshold between insanity and reality. He didn't even have a bad taste in his mouth. Everything he saw and felt, every one of these sensations was undeniably real: the cool door, the digits of the locking mechanism, worn out from frequent use . . . *this damn door in my bedroom!*

Behind the wardrobe.

*It exists. It isn't a dream.*

Or is it?

Leon turned round and looked towards the bed in fear that he would see himself sleeping there, but the sheet was crumpled and the mattress empty. His gaze fell on the camera at his feet, which must have fallen off while he was sleep-walking, and he was reminded of the video. With two quick paces, Leon was back at the laptop and he pressed play again. The sensation of watching a stranger intensified; he almost felt like a voyeur, slightly ashamed and fearfully anticipating what would happen next.

On the monitor Leon watched himself standing in front of the newly exposed door for some time, as if rooted to the spot. As he did nothing but breathe for minutes on end, he decided to speed up the replay, making his reflected persona on the monitor look like a flagpole swaying in the wind. Only after another ten minutes of the video did Leon change his position, and from then on everything happened very quickly. It was over so suddenly that he didn't manage to press pause in time, and he had to rewind it to see it again.

*That's unbelievable*, he thought. Even watching it again,

the events on the laptop monitor lost none of their morbid, schizophrenic fascination.

Initially, it seemed like he was about to make his way back to the bed, for on the recording Leon had turned round. But he glanced up at the bedroom ceiling, then spun back round so quickly that the picture went blurry.

Once the camera's image correction program started functioning again, Leon was already done with the first of the two twist wheels. With practised hand movements, he moved the second into different positions; it all took no longer than a second or two. Then the heavy door seemed to snap open of its own accord, only a few centimetres, but enough for Leon to be able to reach both his hands into the gap and pull it open.

*What's behind it?* The question shot into his mind as he kept his gaze fixed on the laptop screen, trying not to miss a single detail.

Unfortunately, from that moment on there weren't many more images. Everything in Leon was screaming out to discover what lay behind the door; the door that shouldn't really even exist. At the same time, as he watched himself sleepwalking over the threshold, he felt afraid of himself in a way he had never experienced before.

*Where am I going? What's behind the door?*

As Leon stepped through the door in his sleep, he didn't duck down enough to prevent the camera from hitting the doorframe. The device came loose from his head and fell to the floor, where, for just a few seconds, it recorded Leon's back disappearing into the darkness.

Then the film stopped, but Leon still couldn't pull his gaze from the computer.

As though hypnotised, he stared at the monitor until the screensaver eventually washed away the black video window before his watering eyes.

71

Only then did he stir, getting up and walking slowly back to the door in the wall.

'OK, let's think about this rationally,' he said to himself, intertwining his fingers to stop them from trembling. 'If you're not asleep, and you haven't lost your mind, the door must be real. And if it's real . . .'

*. . . it must be possible to open it again.*

He didn't have the strength to utter this last thought out loud.

It didn't take long for an even greater fear to rise up in him, above the realisation that he was leading a double life played out behind closed doors: it was that, in his conscious state, it would be impossible to repeat the movements he had made in his sleep.

In the video he hadn't hesitated for a second, determinedly turning the wheel locks into the necessary positions. Clearly he knew the combination in his sleep.

But *only* in his sleep.

Here and now, he didn't have the slightest idea of what he needed to do to open the locks.

# 12

'A second entrance?'

At the beginning of the telephone conversation the man with the brash voice had sounded merely impatient, but now Benedict Bauer was clearly annoyed. 'What the hell gives you that idea, Herr Nader?'

Leon had prepared a white lie in advance before calling the building custodian. 'We're thinking about renovating our bedroom, and behind the wardrobe there are some markings that I can't find an explanation for.'

One floor above, Michael Tareski was just beginning his daily piano practice. The chemist had discovered his musical passion late in life, and spent at least an hour a day practising the scales.

'I wouldn't want to drill or hammer in a nail in the wrong place,' said Leon, continuing to fib. 'Is it possible that there's something concealed behind the wallpaper?'

'I've got no idea what you're talking about. I gave you the plans when you moved in, remember?'

'Yes, I know,' agreed Leon. At this moment he was sat at his desk in front of the floor plans, which had been included with the rental contract. He'd had to fight for them; originally the custodian did not want to hand them over, presumably to make it more difficult to check the calculation of the rent in the contract against the measurements of the apartment.

'There's no further entrance indicated on my plans . . .'

'There you go then.'

'But perhaps they're not . . .'

'Not complete? Are you implying that we carry out shoddy work?'

'No, of course not . . .'

'But?'

Leon closed his eyes and took a deep breath.

*But there's a door behind the wardrobe in my bedroom, and I have no idea what it's doing there.*

The clumsy piano-playing above his head was getting louder. Leon looked up at the ceiling.

'I really don't mean to cause any trouble, Herr Bauer . . .'

'Good, then I suggest we end this conversation now, otherwise I'm going to miss my train.'

'Yes, of course. Just one last question: is it possible the last tenant changed something without informing you?'

'Rebecca Stahl?' The custodian laughed spitefully. 'I very much doubt it.'

'What makes you so sure?'

'The last tenant was blind. She couldn't even manage to operate the lift, let alone build a new entrance to her bedroom.'

'OK, I see,' said Leon, his tone as flat as his emotions. If he hadn't been sitting down, he would have looked around for a chair.

'Please forgive the interruption,' he said, and was about to hang up when Bauer bluntly asked if something was going on with him.

'You're behaving more and more strangely, Herr Nader. And to be honest the apartment is much too sought-after to be wasted on eccentric tenants.'

74

'What do you mean by eccentric?'

'You've been causing trouble ever since you moved in. First you insisted on being given the floor plans . . .'

'I'm an architect. Those kind of things interest me.'

'Then you bombard me with emails asking to speak to the owner.'

'For the same reason. I've admired the work of Professor von Boyten, who died far too young, ever since my student days, and I would have liked to speak to the son about his genius father . . .'

'Yes, but he didn't want to speak to you. Siegfried von Boyten has never wanted contact with any of his tenants,' said Bauer, letting the second half of his sentence – *and especially not with you* – hang unspoken in the air.

In the background, Leon heard a train station tannoy announcement.

'If you don't change your behaviour, Herr Nader, then I'll have no choice but to dissolve our contract.'

'My behaviour? What's that supposed to mean? Is it against the law to call up the custodian now or something?'

'No. But running around naked in the hallways and frightening other tenants is.'

'I beg your pardon?' asked Leon in confusion, before it occurred to him what the custodian was talking about.

'Oh, I see . . .' he added, not sure what he should say next. *It was only because I was running after my beaten-up wife, because I wanted to stop her leaving me.*

'Spare me the excuses. Instead, turn your attention to clearing all the bicycles, shoes and other objects out of the hallway by the day after tomorrow,' barked Bauer into the phone by way of goodbye.

'Why?'

'Because the renovations on the staircase begin the day

after tomorrow. Maybe you would do better to read the notices instead of studying your floor plans, Herr Nader.'

With that he hung up.

At the same time the piano-playing on the floor above died away too.

# 13

It was a while before Leon dared go back into the bedroom. And yet he didn't know what would be worse: standing in front of the closed metal door in the wall again, or finding the wardrobe in the same position as before, as if it had never been moved.

He delayed the moment by going into the kitchen. Leon hadn't eaten or drunk anything for a long time now, but he was so nervous that he didn't feel hungry or thirsty, even though his stomach was gurgling relentlessly like a central-heating pipe. He wanted to make some tea to calm it down a little, but couldn't find the kettle, which left him wondering why Natalie would bother taking that old, lime-scaled thing.

Once he had taken a drink of water from the tap, his bladder started to press, and he went to the bathroom to relieve himself. Washing his hands, he looked at his face in the mirror. His eyes looked as though he had conjunctivitis. A multitude of burst blood vessels had turned the whites red, providing a strange contrast to the dark shadows beneath them.

He let the water run cold, then splashed some from the basin on to his face. But the enlivening effect he sought failed to materialise, so he leaned over and held his head under the tap.

To begin with he kept his eyes closed, and when he opened them he got such a shock that he jerked his head up, banging his forehead against the tap.

*Damn it, what does this mean?*

The water had washed a tuft of hair from his scalp, but that wasn't what was unsettling him. When he was under emotional stress, he always tended to lose a little hair, but it was just a temporary problem. This time, though, something else had come away with the hair, and it was turning the water into a brown sludge.

Horrified, he ran both his hands through his hair, then stared at his smeared palms.

*How can that that possible?*

He had had a shower yesterday, and now his hair was as dirty as the fur of a dog that had been rolling around on the floor. And it smelled like it, too.

He held a finger in front of his nose and breathed in, and for an instant the smell transported him into a mouldy cellar.

*Where have I been?*

Leon stared at his dirty hands, remembering the earth he had noticed on his socks earlier.

He gave a start and ran back into the bedroom. The mysterious door was still there, the wardrobe pushed aside, and now that he had switched on the ceiling light he could see the specks of dirt he had left on the parquet floor during his nocturnal expedition.

He sat down at the laptop and started the recording from the beginning again. On the very first replay he noticed a peculiarity that he had registered before but not given much thought to: the panning of the camera up. It happened twice. The first time before he heaved the wardrobe to the side in his sleep. The second was just before he opened the mysterious door.

*Why do I keep looking up?*

Leon stood and went over to the approximate spot where he had also stopped on the recording, half a metre from the vault door. Then he craned his head backwards.

At first glance he couldn't make out anything unusual; that is, if you didn't count the hairline fracture that ran across the white-washed plaster. Leon noticed it now for the first time, but for a building of this age such things weren't unusual. It snaked like a crack in the shell of a hard-boiled egg over to a hook in the ceiling. An ugly chandelier had once hung from the hook, a heavy monstrosity that they had got rid of the day they moved in.

The hook, however, had remained, because Natalie wanted to hang an indoor plant or some other decorative object on it to make the room more homely. Directly next to it was a shell-shaped lampshade made of frosted glass, concealing a bulb. For ages he had wanted to replace the shade with a new one that gave out warmer light. Now the sight of it irritated him, even though he couldn't have said why at first look. It was only once he was at the foot of the bed, directly beneath the light, that Leon realised what was bothering him.

He thought it was a speck of dust, then he thought the black fleck inside the glass lamp was a dead insect that had crept through a gap, unseen by the naked eye, and never found its way out again.

In under a minute he had hauled a stepladder out of the small storage space and into the bedroom. Leon placed it under the lamp. He had to leave the room for a second time to fetch his toolbox from the study, then, armed with a screwdriver, he climbed the steps.

Even up close he couldn't make out what was inside the shell. From his new vantage point, standing at the top of the ladder, the glass cover, curved like an eyeball, seemed a lot bigger. And heavier.

Carefully, so the shade didn't fall on him, he began loosening the four thick screws holding the lamp to the ceiling. As he did so, he noticed signs of wear and tear on the screw-heads. One screw was quite loose, while the last initially refused to budge at all. Only with a great deal of force did he manage to unscrew it, and then Leon made a grave mistake, letting the screwdriver slip from his grasp, and, as he tried to grab it, he began to teeter. So as not to follow suit behind the tool, he had to let go of the lamp, which meant its entire weight hung on only the last screw. Of course, it didn't hold for long.

The shade lurched to the side, wrenching out the screw, and fell, shattering as it hit the floor.

*Shit.*

Cursing, Leon climbed down from the ladder and knelt on the parquet to search the shards for the contents of the shell. But given that he didn't know what he was looking for, he didn't hold out great hopes of finding it.

He needed to gather up the shards anyway, piece by piece, and as carefully and thoroughly as possible so that he wouldn't cut himself later. Luckily, the shade had broken into several large pieces, of which two had shot so far under the bed that Leon decided to leave them there. The other pieces he stacked on top of one another like fruit bowls, with the intention of fetching a plastic bag and the vacuum cleaner. But he didn't get to that, instead picking up the smallest shard, carefully and with his fingertips, for this piece had the sharpest edges.

*What in God's name . . .?*

He turned the shard over and looked at the object, curved like a contact lens and filed off at the edges, still clinging to the glass from its underside.

*What is it?*

Morphet shot into Leon's mind. The thing had a surface

structure and consistency that wasn't unlike the cockroach's shell, albeit a different colour. At close proximity it was clear that it came from a human hand. Dry blood crusted the underside of the keratin plate.

'A fingernail?' whispered Leon, hoping he was wrong. It was painted a mud-like colour and had been extracted almost completely intact. But there could be no doubt as to whose thumb it once belonged to.

# 14

Volwarth had once compared the subconscious to the deep sea. The further down you go, the greater the danger of being crushed by its strength, and if you surface again too quickly, your head could explode.

Leon looked at the torn-off thumbnail, sensing that he was only at the beginning of a long dive. He had put his head under the water just once, and already he had made unimaginable discoveries, of which the door in the wall behind the wardrobe was definitely the most disturbing.

He turned the nail over, from lacquered, manicured surface to its underside, which until recently had still been united with his wife's thumb. At the sight of the encrusted blood underneath, the thought of how much pain Natalie must have suffered made him close his eyes and take a deep breath.

He looked at the nail again, and only now, on the second glance, did he notice the details. On the underside blood had crusted, but lower down, barely visible to the naked eye, the surface seemed a little too even.

Leon opened his toolbox and took out a halogen torch. Not able to see much more even with that, he reached for a Swiss pocket knife, which contained a little magnifying glass. The magnification wasn't perfect, but it was enough to be able to make out punctures on the nail. With a tiny object, someone had scratched a series of numbers into the encrusted blood.

'*One, two, zero ...*' whispered Leon. He broke out in a cold sweat and his heart seemed to stop for a second, his neck and calf muscles cramping up as if he was preparing to take flight. The final number – a four – a little offset and barely decipherable in the second row, completed his birth date: the twelfth of April.

Slowly, but with his pulse racing, he turned to the door in the wall.

*Is it possible that . . .*

He stood up to check his suspicion. It suddenly felt a lot warmer than it had a few minutes ago, even though the heating in the bedroom had been turned down to the lowest setting, because Natalie preferred to sleep with an open window and temperature of sixteen degrees. Leon, on the other hand, needed absolute quiet at night and insisted on closed windows and doors, even though there wasn't much street noise in this neighbourhood anyway. Turning down the heating had been their compromise.

Abrupt sadness eclipsed his tense, fearful nervousness as he stood before the vault door, the thumbnail clasped in his fist. He tried with all his might to suppress thoughts of Natalie, but the tighter he balled his fist, the stronger his conviction became that he might never again get the opportunity to squabble with his wife over the temperature in the bedroom.

*A relationship is a battle*, his mother had once said to him, meaning it in a positive sense. *It's not fighting that poisons a marriage, but indifference.*

'I hope you were right,' said Leon, continuing his whispered monologue as he moved the uppermost of the two wheel locks on the door. Because based on how things looked right now, it was not indifference, but a brutal fight that had torn Natalie and him apart.

*A fight to the death?*

Leon turned in a clockwise direction until the '1' was beneath the marking arrow above the cogwheel. At once he felt the locking mechanism react to the position into which he had turned the wheel. The click that swiftly followed as he turned the wheel to '2' confirmed his theory. And once Leon had turned the second wheel to the numbers '0' and '4', forming the month of his birth date, the same thing happened that he had witnessed on the video recording: *click!*

The vault door sprang open.

Leon's initial reaction was irrational. He looked around the bedroom, as if for any witnesses to this unbelievable event. Once he had assured himself that he was still alone, he stretched his fingers out, worried that they would be crushed the very second he laid them in the gap around the door.

*I can't believe I'm really doing this.*

It moved more easily than he expected for a door of its weight, as the hinges were well greased. As soon as he had it completely open, the air turned colder, and this time it wasn't his overwrought psyche playing tricks on him. Cool air was streaming into the bedroom through the dark opening in the wall.

It was stale and smelled of paint, reminding him of the tool cellar where his father had always built the Carrera track at Christmas. And it also smelled like the dirt he had washed out of his hair earlier. Leon squinted and tilted his head to the side, but even as he moved closer, he could only make out the black-painted walls of a small room that didn't seem to have any floor.

It was as though he had opened the portal to a black hole.

He reached for the torch again and, keeping his distance from the door, shone it into the darkness. It wasn't a wise decision.

For beyond the threshold there really was no floor, just an abyss, *opening up like the jaws of a beast of prey*, as Leon suddenly thought. He even thought he could make out the teeth, stretching back into the neck of this supernatural being. In reality they were just the rungs of a ladder set into the brickwork, leading deeper and deeper down into the darkness.

Out of fear that an ill-advised movement might make him lose balance, Leon knelt and shone the torch down into the shaft, which was spherical. The beam became thinner and thinner, not reaching the bottom. The walls were rough and uneven, and here and there black-painted bricks jutted out of the chute, which became increasingly narrow as it stretched down.

*And I climbed down this in the night?*

Leon thought back to the self-assuredness he had observed in his sleepwalking self. The schizophrenic feeling of being in another body during his conscious state intensified.

His knees trembling, he stood up and made the decision to sort through the facts calmly before going any further.

*There must be a logical explanation for all of this.*

For Natalie's injuries. The trainers. The thumbnail.

*For the door.*

Dr Volwarth had said that he was fine. That he wasn't violent. But Dr Volwarth had seen neither the video nor the shaft, opening up in his bedroom like a portal to another world.

A shaft, from which cold cellar air was still streaming.

Along with a noise that Leon had heard many times in his life, and which was getting louder every second.

*That's impossible*, he thought, creeping back towards the

85

vault door. Once again he directed the beam of the torchlight down into the abyss, which wasn't actually necessary, because the classical melody had its own light source: a display that was blinking in rhythm with the tinkling sound.

'Natalie,' cried Leon, pressing his hand over his mouth.

His wife's mobile phone, which she had been holding when she left the house a few days ago, lay at the foot of the shaft and was ringing non-stop.

# 15

In the end it happened despite all his attempts to prevent it. He fell.

Leon had, however, been sensible enough to pull on the work overalls he wore for site visits. His fingers, gripping the metal rungs, were clad in his work gloves, and thanks to the thick rubber soles on his steel-capped boots, his feet were sure not to slip.

He had attached the torch to the tool belt of his overalls so that it shone straight down, even though as he climbed he was avoiding looking into the depths. Step by step, rung by rung, he fumbled his way down towards the mobile phone, which had stopped ringing as soon as he crossed the threshold of the door.

It wasn't long before he had descended more than halfway. Even though it was getting cooler with every metre, beads of sweat were gathering on his forehead. He tried to ignore it, but it got worse so he stopped to wipe the back of his hands across his eyes.

It happened as he was descending the last third. By now Leon had developed a method; he knew how far down to stretch his right leg to reach the next rung, how far he had to go before his foot would reach the step and he was able to release his left hand and bring it down so that it could grip the next rung, after which this succession of movements could be repeated with his left leg and right hand. Leon felt sure he could do the last few metres with his eyes closed if he needed to, and it was this mistaken belief that was his downfall.

Several things happened at once: Leon heard a light knocking that seemed to be coming from his apartment's front door above, just as his foot stepped into nothingness. For the first time the space between the rungs had changed, if only slightly. He didn't have a foothold, and then the phone beneath him began to ring again.

With the unmistakable classical ringtone that Natalie had only recently picked, except this time much louder.

Leon gave such a start that he released his right hand – too quickly. He literally jumped down to the next rung. And by chance this one had been either badly made, weakened by age or, for some reason or other, not securely fastened to the wall. As soon as Leon's foot landed on it, he knew the rung wouldn't hold his weight. By then it was too late.

He just had time to grip one hand around the metal strut, cushioning his fall a little. But he still ended up swinging to the side like a window shutter and banging his hip against a protruding brick, causing his torch to come loose from the belt and fall. He didn't hear the glass shatter because of the phone ringing, but the fact that the beam of light was immediately extinguished spoke for itself.

'Shit!' cried Leon into the darkness. Only the weakly flickering phone display was still casting light across the floor, like a glow worm.

It took him almost as long to descend the last section as it had the whole preceding stretch, because he didn't want to make another mistake. By the time he finally felt solid ground under his feet, the telephone had long since gone silent, as had the knocking on the apartment door, and it took Leon a while to find the phone on the dry floor, which was covered by a thick blanket of dust.

In the process he stirred up so much dirt that he sneezed, which down here sounded like a small explosion. The sound was reflected by the brickwork, then amplified and sent back as a dull echo. With these acoustics, no wonder the ringing of the phone had been so loud. Even a gentle cough sounded like the crack of a whip.

*Where in God's name am I?*

Leon snapped the mobile open and gasped for air. When he saw the photo used as the background, he knew he was holding Natalie's phone in his hands. It was a portrait of her, one of those typical snapshots that people take of themselves, head thrown back, mouth stretched into a broad smile, all in hope that the outstretched hand was at such an angle that the camera wouldn't cut off the forehead or only capture the upper body.

*First the identity bracelet in the fixing bath. Now the mobile phone down here. Natalie, what happened?*

Leon erased the message announcing sixteen missed calls and several voicemails. Most were from him. The other incoming calls, including the last, had been dialled from a withheld number.

For a mobile phone, the illumination from the display was surprisingly strong, but it wasn't enough to give him a good look at this mysterious place. In spite of the anxiety gripping him, Leon tried to approach things systematically. He imagined the floor of the shaft as a clockface, and made a mark in the dust directly in front of the wall, as twelve o'clock. Using it as a starting point, he groped his way along the brickwork, until, after a three-quarter-turn to around nine o'clock, he stumbled into another rung. At first glance it didn't seem to serve any purpose, for he couldn't make out any further struts above it. So it wasn't another way up.

Leon put the mobile in the breast pocket of his overalls and gave the strut a shake. It moved, and for a second he thought he had pulled it off the wall, but the weight in his hands was too heavy for that. As he heard a creaking sound, he realised he had just found another door.

This was made of plywood, not metal like the one above, and so was much easier to move. Thanks also to it being not much bigger than the door to a dog kennel, as Leon could see when he shone the mobile on it again.

He held his arm out in front of him as far as possible to illuminate the tunnel beyond the newly discovered opening. Given that the entrance was small, he imagined the passageway would be the same, but when he shone the phone up, the light met no resistance – if he could squeeze through the gateway he would be able to stand up in the room beyond it.

*But do I want to?*

Leon looked up the shaft to the light from his bedroom, feeling as though he had been buried alive, with only weak signals from the outside world making their way through.

He stood up and shook the rungs of the ladder – apart from the one on which he had lost his balance, they were firmly attached to the brickwork. So he shouldn't have any problems getting back up, as long as he didn't get lost down here.

*And it seems I know the way even in my sleep.*

The voice of reason inside his head was screaming at him to climb back up and fetch help. But what if something awful had happened down here? Something he had been involved in?

*Something I'm responsible for?*

Leon knew that feeling, and he couldn't ignore it any more. Much like the flu, it had begun with symptoms that could be suppressed at first, but which ultimately end up

90

seizing the entire body in an iron grip: he was afraid. Afraid of a real person who was lurking down here and who he had never before encountered in his life, even though they had always been in close proximity. He was afraid of himself. Of his other, sleeping self.

For this reason, ironically it ended up being the voice of cowardice that stopped him from contacting the building management, Sven, Dr Volwarth or even the police.

Leon wanted to find out what was waiting for him down here before he fetched back-up. And as he crept head first through the narrow entrance into the darkness, he was already fearing the worst.

# 16

It was the barely noticeable smell of fresh washing that made Leon come to an abrupt halt. From one second to the next, he was no longer in the world between worlds that he had stepped into through his wardrobe but back in his childhood.

He had been ten years old at the time, his surname still Wieler, when his biological father Roman first told him about the Ghosts of the Twelve Nights. Sarah Wieler had rebuked her husband considerably for this after finding out. She was of the opinion that such horror stories were not for children of Leon's age, that they would only make his night terrors worse. And she was right. That same night Leon had nightmares about the ghosts being in his wardrobe, and of the misfortune they had already brought upon many a family.

'Do you know why your mama doesn't do any washing between Christmas and New Year?' Roman had asked, by way of beginning the story. Leon had instinctively grabbed his father's hand, as if in fear that the answer alone could cause him to stumble.

Whenever he thought back to that day, as he did now, on all fours in the darkness, every detail of that Sunday stroll came rushing back: the cold wind in his face, the snow under his boots, their gloved, interlinked fingers, the Christmas decorations in the windows of the neighbouring houses.

'I'm guessing you've never heard about the Ghosts of the Twelve Nights, have you? They hide themselves away all year, and there's just one time when they dare to venture out. And that time is coming. The Twelve Nights; that's what we call the time between Christmas and New Year.'

'What do the ghosts do?' Leon wanted to know.

His father nodded as though he had asked a particularly clever question.

'They are the opposite of guardian angels. Misfortune befalls the houses they live in. And during these days they are on the search for new families.'

'Will they come to us, too?'

'Only if we use the washing machine. Not many people know this, but these ghosts need wet washing to survive. They creep into the wet bed-sheets, into your socks or trousers, and once everything is dry they cling there for a year.'

To this day Leon still didn't know where in the world this superstition came from, but in the days that followed that walk he had scrupulously made sure his clothes didn't go anywhere near the laundry. And he was horrified when, on New Year's Eve, he found his older sister's blouses hanging on the washing line. She had laughed at him when he begged her to remove the wet shirts from the house immediately. From that day on he lived in the irrational certainty of a ten-year-old convinced his bedroom had been seized by evil spirits. His parents' attempts to reassure him were all in vain.

It was months before he stopped insisting his mother check under the bed or in the wardrobe after turning out the lights, to see if a ghost might be hiding there. The night of the seventh of May was the first that Leon no longer gave any thought to the Twelve Nights, having calmed down by then. He could remember the date so precisely because it was the night before the accident.

*Fate?*

Leon was shivering with cold; because of his rigid stance on the hard ground it had penetrated his limbs. He shook himself free from his memory-filled paralysis. Ever since the accident he had refused to do washing between Christmas and New Year. This made it all the more disturbing to him that here, of all places, he was confronted with the scent of softener and detergent. Whoever was responsible for it clearly didn't know the legend of the Twelve Nights.

*Or they are ignoring it.*

Leon activated the display of the mobile again, for the screensaver had vanished into the darkness, and saw that he didn't need to crawl any longer. The subtle scent of washing had disappeared too, or maybe Leon just couldn't smell it any more on account of the fact that his senses were focused on figuring out his new surroundings.

The passageway stretching out in front of him looked like a mining tunnel that had been carved into the rock with some blunt device. Pitch-black, uneven walls made a channel of varying size. Even over his head the height kept changing, and he had to stretch his hand out to prevent himself from banging into a sharp edge.

The ground beneath his feet felt strange. As Leon walked along, it gave a little like a forest path and when he knelt down, he was able to dislodge some earth. The path sloped downwards, intensifying the unsettling sensation of approaching an underworld that it would be better not to enter.

The tension mounted with every step, and became so intense he was convinced he could feel a subtle vibration spreading through his whole body. He wasn't claustrophobic, but right now he could easily imagine how it felt to be one of those people who avoid enclosed spaces. Whenever the light on the mobile cut out, and he found himself in complete darkness for a split second, it was as though the blackness hit him in the face. He could feel his heart hammering in his chest and the blood rushing in his veins, and his mouth become dry.

'Natalie?' he called tentatively. He had made it to the end of the passageway and found himself before a fork in the path. Calling his wife's name probably had an equally slim chance of success as trying to navigate the tunnel system down here by himself. But what else was he supposed to do? Go back upstairs? Call Volwarth? Or the building management?

He came to the conclusion that this probably wasn't as bad an idea as he had initially thought. At least he now had proof of a second entrance to his bedroom, one that for some reason hadn't been included in the floor plans.

But who put it there? And why? And what was Natalie's phone doing down here?

Leon shone the light to the right, into the shorter part of the fork. After just a few steps the path ended at a wall on which hung a warning sign: 'DANGER' was written in old-fashioned script, directly above an image of a lightning bolt as warning of high voltage.

Leon decided to contact Dr Volwarth before doing anything else; this would give him a witness who could testify that he wasn't hallucinating. But then he realised the psychiatrist would be on the plane now, well on his way to Tokyo.

He still wanted to turn back, out of fear of getting lost down here. Who knew how many forks might be lying ahead? He had stumbled into a labyrinth. After all, the architect of the building, Albert von Boyten, had also been known as a landscape artist, whose artfully created mazes attracted international renown. Did he give this building a maze too, albeit one made of stone rather than tall hedges?

Leon called his wife's name again before he turned to leave, but then something happened that stopped him from heading back: he suddenly realised that he had been mistaken. The vibration that he had put down to a trick of the senses was real. It existed – and not inside, but outside his body, and now he could not just feel it, but *hear* it too.

Leon tilted his head to the side and took a step towards the sound – the longer of the forked paths. The light of the phone's display had a greenish tinge, which made it even harder to see. If Leon wasn't mistaken, the walls in this part of the tunnel were smooth and even.

He put his hands out to touch the sides, tentatively, as though he might be electrocuted: to his left, he felt an even surface. To his right, the brickwork was clad with some coarse material.

With every step, the background noise became louder. Leon suspected that an inaudible, deep bass was causing the regular vibrations coming from the walls.

*And what the hell is . . . that?*

He had only gone a few metres before he stumbled upon a door handle.

Leon held the mobile up, and discovered he was right. There really was a door built into the right-hand side of the passageway – all the more disturbing was how incredibly normal it looked.

He pressed down on the handle, which was astonishingly warm to the touch, and expected to hear a creaking or squeaking, but the door opened almost silently. In the very same breath, the sounds around Leon died down and the vibrations ebbed away.

Clearly the door was used often, for the hinges were well oiled.

The room he entered was barely bigger than Natalie's dark room, and reminded him of the plywood crates every tenant had been given as cellar space, and which you needed to put your bicycle into upended so that it fit.

Leon's next thought was that he had stumbled into some homeless person's night-time shelter. The light from the mobile revealed a threadbare mattress on the floor, a half-opened removal box and several plastic bags, the contents of which he was reluctant to investigate. Judging by the smell, they contained rotting food products and other household waste.

Leon's foot became entangled with a scrunched-up sheet. As he bent down to remove it, he saw the box was full of objects, one of which he recognised.

*But that's impossible . . .*

He reached for the kettle that he had been searching for earlier in his kitchen. To Leon's astonishment, it was full to the first marker, as though it had been used down here not so long ago.

*But that doesn't make any sense.*

Leon looked around for a power point. Right next to the door, he saw a multi socket in the wall. A small, familiar-looking table lamp had been plugged into it. It was a cheap one, without a shade or base, nothing more than a bulb attached to a pliable stem. Unless he was mistaken, Natalie had used it in her flat-share as a bedside lamp, and had never unpacked it from the box after they moved in together.

He flipped on the switch. The bulb lit up, if only weakly, a scene that made Leon doubt his sanity more and more.

To his right, next to the door, there was an old garden chair with a rusted frame. The seat had been covered with the catalogue from an electronics store, under which there was a cigar-shaped bulge.

Leon formed his index finger and thumb into a pincer

97

and pulled the catalogue from the chair, revealing a pile of white paper, the kind he used in his study for architectural drawings. And on the top, right in the middle of a sheet, was the *fountain pen*! The graduation present from his adoptive father which he had been looking for on the telephone table so that Volwarth could make out the prescription. Speechless, Leon stared at the golden pen, its nib pointing at him like a compass needle. He picked it up, revealing a column of figures noted carefully on the paper, which until then had been hidden by the pen.

Guessing it to be a phone number, Leon tapped it into Natalie's mobile so he could look it up later, but before he had entered the last digit he froze in shock. Natalie's phone had recognised the number. It was saved as a contact, and Leon was just as unable to explain this as he was the circumstances that led him down into this hiding place.

*Dr Volwarth?*

What was his psychiatrist's number doing in his wife's mobile phone?

Clueless, he stared at the carefully input address details.

He and Natalie had talked many times about the sleep disturbances of his childhood, and he was sure to have mentioned the name of the doctor who had treated him back then, but that still didn't explain why she would have the address of Dr Volwarth's practice, his email address and even an emergency telephone number.

*Were the two of them in contact?*

Under normal circumstances he would have looked for a logical, harmless explanation. But, down here, things were neither normal nor logical.

*And they certainly aren't harmless.*

He studied the hiding place more closely in the light of the lamp. He paused. Held his breath, tried to stay calm. And looked at the floor again.

What he thought was a bed-sheet, the thing he had stumbled over . . . was in fact something much worse.

He leaned over and grabbed at the material, which felt soft, as though it had just been washed – then he saw the rust-coloured flecks that had seeped into the cotton's flower design where the smooth material became ruffled.

Leon closed his eyes, and the image of Natalie kneeling in front of the wardrobe and cramming her things into the suitcase shot back into his mind. The memory of her flight from the apartment had imprinted itself in his head like a tyre track in wet concrete. He felt sure he would be able to recall every detail of this scene, again and again, to the very end of his life, even the insignificant things – for example, what top Natalie had been wearing: the flower-patterned one with the ruffled sleeves.

*Natalie? Where are you?*

Leon was about to bury his face in the material, to inhale his wife's scent, insofar as it was still present and not overpowered by other smells (*cellar, blood, fear*) – but then the light went out.

There was a soft *clink*, indicating that the lamp's bulb had blown, and this, combined with the unexpected plunge into darkness, startled Leon so much that he dropped the phone.

He fumbled around on the dusty floor for it. The oppressive fear that he would never find his way out of this underworld again was almost overpowering him when, there in the darkness, something brushed against Leon.

# 17

Leon yelled out, jumping at the sound of his own voice. He hit out at his trouser leg where he had felt as though someone was trying to grab hold of him. As he did, his fingers touched the mobile he thought he had lost. He clasped his fingers tightly around it as though it were a dumbbell.

The battery made a beeping sound to announce that it was now at under 20 per cent as he activated the display for the umpteenth time, convinced that it would light up a grotesque face with bleeding eyes. He was expecting a wide-open jaw and fangs just centimetres away from his face, ready to bite, chew, swallow.

But all he saw was the open door.

*I have to get out of here!*

Leon pulled himself to his feet and stumbled out of the room. Without stopping to think, he ran in the wrong direction, away from the fork that would have led him back to the ladder.

After a few metres he stumbled into a stone ledge and stopped to look around, but there was nothing but the impenetrable blackness of the passageway. Leon's thoughts were racing as quickly as his pulse. He needed to get back upstairs fast, without having to pass the room again. Only now did he realise he still had the blood-smeared blouse in his hands. His fingers had cramped up around the material. He stuffed it into his overalls, then talked himself into going back the way he had come. If he didn't, the danger of getting lost would be too great. And if there really was something down here lying in wait for him, it could be anywhere; it wouldn't necessarily be waiting in that room to jump out at him.

Then there was a rustling sound. Right next to him.

*It's just some animal. A rat, perhaps. Or Morphet,* he tried to reassure himself, but in vain. His survival instinct was stronger than his sense of reason.

Leon edged away, turned and ran, crashing into a wall and completely losing his sense of orientation. The only thing he had to go on was the rustling behind his back, which had now become a loud scraping, one he wanted to get as far away from as possible. But the noise grew louder the further he stumbled along the passageway, the contours of which he was only able to guess at in the weak gleam coming from the mobile.

Suddenly, a jolting pain shot through his shoulder, forcing him to stop. He looked at the thing he had run into, and recognised the metal rungs in the wall. It vibrated like a tuning fork as he grabbed it. Then he heard the rustling sound behind him again, louder and nearer, and in that second Leon realised there were two different sounds hunting him. They were coming from different directions. As they slowly made their way towards him, a metallic scraping sound droned above his head, albeit from a considerable distance. To Leon, it seemed less alive and therefore less dangerous.

Once he had discovered a second rung in the brickwork at head height, he didn't hesitate for one more second.

He made his way upwards hand over hand, and this time it was the ascent that would lead him into the unknown.

# 18

Rung by rung, Leon climbed towards the din, and rung by rung he became increasingly unsure that he had made the right decision. It wasn't just the droning, scraping and stamping – the vibrations, too, were becoming stronger.

But the irrational fear of what was behind him and the hope of escaping this labyrinth of darkness drove him on.

The way up seemed instinctively more promising than staying down there in the cellar.

His arms were sore and becoming heavier with every bar he grasped, but he forced himself to keep up the pace and even quicken it. Then, sooner than expected, he collided with the top of the shaft.

In shock, he almost let go of the last rung. He didn't even want to think about what could have happened if he had fallen backwards into the darkness. If the shaft was as deep as the one he had discovered behind his wardrobe, he would have broken his spine or neck. Probably both.

And if the obstacle he had crashed into above had not given way a little, the collision would have been much more painful.

Slowly, Leon stretched his left hand upwards, but the trapdoor on top of the shaft was very heavy. He hunched his back and climbed further up to try to lift it with his shoulders. He braced himself against it, feeling like he was carrying a sack of coals on his back. In reality, he was opening a trapdoor, which tipped to the side with a clatter as Leon climbed up into a room.

Visibly, there was no great change. Wherever he was, he was still in almost complete darkness. He could see just two soft LED lights hovering at the end of the room, reminding him of the lights on the USB stick of his laptop.

Leon, wheezing now, lay flat on his stomach on the floor. It was pleasantly cool.

Then he smelled the scent he had caught just a whiff of in the labyrinth, and all of a sudden he knew where he was and what had caused the vibrating noise. The noise that had stopped briefly at the moment he opened the trapdoor, and which was now shaking the floor again just as loudly as before.

Leon propped himself on all fours, crept over the cold tiles to the wall and pulled himself up to a standing position. He took Natalie's mobile from his overalls and, shining the light around the room, confirmed his suspicion: he was in a bathroom, a completely normal one.

To his right was a washbasin, next to it a bathtub, and inside that an open and fully laden clothes horse. Between the washbasin and the tub, a bulky washing machine was just finishing its spin cycle.

Leon was wondering who it belonged to, and whose apartment he had unintentionally stumbled into, when outside the bathroom the hallway light went on.

# 19

'Where are you, my darling?'

Ivana Helsing stood in the doorway in her dressing gown, both hands on her bony hips, sweeping her gaze around the bathroom.

'Have you hidden yourself away in here?'

She hadn't noticed the hole in her bathroom floor (*at least, not yet*), for Leon had just managed to shut the trap-door in time and pull the rug over it. His neighbour must have heard the noise, even if it had been drowned out to a great extent by the roar of the washing machine. The hiding place he had found was so poor that Leon expected to be discovered at any second. He had jumped into the bathtub almost as Ivana walked into the bathroom, and now stood on trembling legs between the wall and the clothes horse. He had pulled the shower curtain hastily across, and even this seemed to have escaped the old woman's attention. Clearly she was more interested in where her cat was hiding.

'Alba, where are you this time?'

Peeping around the shower curtain, Leon shot a quick glance at the mirror over the sink, and saw Ivana pulling a little metal box from the pocket of her dressing gown.

'Come on, my darling,' she called, shaking the dry cat food. 'I have some delicious treats here for you.'

She positioned herself next to the washing machine.

'Alba? Can you hear me?'

She rattled the box again, but the animal showed no sign of revealing itself. She put the box back into her pocket.

Leon watched Ivana walk over to the mirror and take off her glasses. Then she blinked, as though she had a speck of dust in her eye. She seemed to be fighting back tears.

'She's just like you, Richard,' she whispered, barely audible now. 'She always leaves me alone.'

Leon's senses were stretched to breaking point. He was stood in an uncomfortable position, one hand pressed against the wall, the other stopping the clothes horse from falling over. He was breathing shallowly and trying not to make any noise, but as soon as this next thought occurred to him (*Hopefully I won't need to sneeze!*), he felt a prickling sensation in his nose.

Ivana was studying her face in the mirror. She massaged the sizeable bags under her eyes, shook her head and pulled her wrinkled skin down over her jaw. Then she checked her hair, which was grey but still thick, but she didn't seem satisfied even with that.

'Everyone leaves me,' she whispered, turning the tap on. 'They always do.'

Leon felt the muscles in his back tensing up. He wouldn't be able to hold this position much longer, but how could he explain himself if a careless movement revealed his presence?

He could only hope that Ivana would hurry up. But she seemed unwilling to do him this favour, because she began to take her clothes off – even though there wasn't very much that she could take off.

First she pulled the dressing gown down over her drooping, slightly forward-curving shoulders. As she was wearing neither a top nor a bra, Leon could see her breasts in the mirror. They were saturated with liver spots and hung over her ribs like half-deflated air balloons.

Leon felt ashamed for this unwitting, intimate insight his neighbour had granted him. And yet he couldn't bring himself to turn away; not even when Ivana Helsing lifted up her varicose-vein-covered legs, one after the other, to take off her nude-coloured pants.

Leon had never before seen a naked woman of this age (he was guessing she was in her late seventies), but it was not her nakedness that had seized his attention, it was the tattoo on her back: two blue snakes wound themselves around her spine like a DNA helix, their heads turned towards each other on her bony shoulders, the sharp tongues knotting together into a kiss on her neck.

Ivana began to wash herself with a flannel, first her face, then her neck, and finally her breasts, and as she did so Leon's nose itched more and more. The smell of clean washing made him think back to the legend of the Twelve Nights for a moment, which made the bizarre situation even more real. All of a sudden, Ivana began to sob loudly, and she threw the wet flannel against the mirror in anger.

'You piece of shit,' she cried out. Then she grabbed her dressing gown again and shuffled out of the bathroom without turning off the light.

Leon's urge to sneeze disappeared with Ivana. He waited a while. Only when he heard the TV being switched on in the living room did he finally dare to leave his hiding place.

The apartment was laid out just like his: the corridor beyond the bathroom went left into the living room; on the right-hand side to the hallway, and the front door leading out into the stairwell just a few steps away. But there was a problem. Unlike his apartment, just one floor above, this one hadn't been renovated for years. This was evident not just from the yellowing wallpaper and partially loose skirting boards, but also from the floorboards that creaked loudly with every movement.

Hoping that the TV would be just as good an acoustic distraction as the washing machine, Leon crept out to the front door, and he probably would have made it past her unnoticed, had the telephone not rung.

The green phone with its old-fashioned rotary dial was right next to him, on a crocheted coaster, on the edge of a teak commode.

Looking around in desperation, Leon hesitated, before diving into the small room by the front door, which in his flat would have been his study. Down here the door had been removed, and the room was completely empty apart from a small removals box.

*There's nowhere I can hide*, he thought, as the phone stopped ringing. And as he heard the shocked voice of Ivana Helsing behind him.

# 20

'Herr Nader?'

Leon whipped around and saw a nervous-looking woman standing opposite him, fiddling anxiously with the belt of her dressing gown. Her glasses were a little foggy and her face was still wet from her tears. She was wearing polka-dot slippers, the joints of her knobbly toes pressing into the material.

Leon felt there was only one way he could get away with this.

'What are you doing here, Frau Helsing?'

'Me?' she asked in astonishment. She smiled nervously.

'Yes, what are you doing in my apartment?'

'In *your* apartment?' Her smile took on a tortured look.

Leon could almost feel her inner conflict. On the one hand, she knew him as her pleasant, unassuming neighbour. But on the other hand, she was afraid of finding out why he had suddenly appeared out of nowhere and was talking nonsense. And in that get-up! After all, he was standing before her in dusty overalls, his hair dripping with sweat and plastered to his face, his hands covered in dirt.

Leon's thoughts raced. Simply telling the truth (*I found a door behind my wardrobe through which I climb down into a shaft when I'm sleepwalking, and I got lost and ended up in your bathroom*) certainly wouldn't be of much help in defusing the situation.

If he said that, of course, he would need to prove it and show her the hatch in her bathroom. But until he knew what he had unleashed down there in the labyrinth (that was what he had christened the world behind the walls), he didn't want to confide in anyone else.

'Can I help you in some way, Frau Helsing?' said Leon, continuing his charade, then he glanced into the empty room on the left and feigned a surprised expression. 'Wait a moment, I . . .'

He inspected his surroundings like an actor stepping into unknown territory. Then he held his hand up in front of his mouth. 'My God, I . . . I . . . Oh, this is very embarrassing. I'm afraid that I've . . .'

'You've . . . what?'

'Got lost.'

'Excuse me?'

'Yes, I went downstairs to fetch the post and when I came back up the steps I was lost in thought. Your front door was open, and I must have thought I was already on the third floor, because I left my front door ajar too. Frau Helsing, I don't know what to say . . .'

He let the last sentence hang in the air, searching the old woman's face for a sign that she had bought his cock and bull story.

'My front door was open?' asked Ivana, not one jot less suspicious.

'Yes, I know how it sounds, but I'm working on a big project right now, a commission I have to finish in the next few days, and whenever I think about some of the problems with it, it's like I'm in another world.'

Leon began to sweat; he was aware that his story, like every good lie, had truth at the heart of it.

Ivana Helsing shook her head in disbelief and stepped sideways to look past him to the front door. Her expression darkened when she saw the chain was on.

*Damn it.*

'I don't believe it . . .' she said softly.

'I know it sounds crazy, but—'

'I don't believe this has happened yet again.'

'Again?' Now it was Leon's turn to be confused.

Ivana sighed and rubbed one of her eyes, without taking off her glasses. 'I've already spoken to my doctor about my forgetfulness, you see. He says it's nothing to worry about, not Alzheimer's or dementia or anything like that. Just the normal deterioration of the body as the years pass.' She shook her head again. 'But it scares me, Leon. I forget the simplest things. Like to drink enough water, for example. I should drink much more. And at night I sometimes leave the TV on. And Alba is always dashing past me through the door. You didn't see her, by any chance, did you?'

'No,' said Leon. 'But don't worry. Forgetfulness isn't necessarily connected to age,' he added, trying to ease the situation. 'I mean, which of us is in the wrong apartment right now?'

She couldn't help but laugh, and at once much of the tension fell away.

'I'm really very sorry, and I promise it won't happen again, Frau Helsing.'

'Wait a moment, please,' she called as he turned to go.

'Yes?'

'I've just put some tea on.' Shyly, she gestured towards the living room behind her. 'Won't you keep me company just a little, now that you're here?'

She reached for his hand, seemingly unbothered by the dirt. 'Please stay just a little.'

'That's really very sweet of you,' Leon protested, 'but as

110

I said, I'm right in the middle of this pitch for an architec-tural project, and I . . .'

As he shook her hand, his gaze fell on a set of armchairs grouped around an open fire in the living room. Over the fireplace hung an immense oil painting.

He stopped.

'Is something wrong?' asked Ivana, nervous again, turning to follow the direction of Leon's rigid gaze.

'Yes,' he said absent-mindedly, letting go of her hand and walking into the sitting room, intrigued.

'What's wrong? Are you feeling unwell?'

'Excuse me?' Leon blinked. 'Oh, no, nothing's wrong. I'm just wondering about . . . this picture.'

He pointed above the fireplace, suddenly feeling dazed again.

'Yes, what about it?'

'The man, the portrait, isn't that . . .?'

'Albert von Boyten? Yes.'

'You knew the architect who designed this building?' Leon turned to look at her.

'Yes,' smiled Ivana, a little mischievously this time, and all at once the spark she must have had in her younger years was reignited. 'For many years I was his lover.'

# 21

Leon sat opposite her on a chair from which, moments ago, he had cleared a pile of women's magazines and crossword books, setting them on the coffee table.

Ivana sat bolt upright, without touching the chair's backrest and taking care that the hem of her dressing gown didn't come over her pressed-together knees.

'I'm really sorry about your wife, by the way,' she said as she poured Leon a cup of the steaming tea.

He tensed.

'It's the building, you know. If you'd spoken to me before you moved in, I would have warned you.'

'About what?'

She put the teapot back on a coaster and interlaced her fingers on her lap, the tips of her thumbs drumming against one another and reminding Leon of the heads of the kissing snakes on her back.

'It has eyes, you know. The house, I mean. Don't you often feel as though you're being watched? Sometimes I wake up in the night and feel like there's someone sat on my bed. I turn the light on, and of course there's never anyone there, but I just can't get rid of the feeling. Sometimes I even look in the cupboard, such a silly goose, and can only go back to sleep again once I've assured myself that there's no one there.'

She shook her head as she spoke – as older people have a tendency to do without realising – and Leon hoped that it wasn't an early sign of Parkinson's.

'My God, you must think I'm a crazy old bat.'

'No, not in the slightest,' replied Leon, anxiously recalling how he had spied on her in the bathroom just a few minutes ago. Then he remembered the clothes horse, the wet sheets hanging on it, the Twelve Nights they were currently in, and the ghosts that were on the hunt for a new home.

He took a sip of tea and tried to concentrate on the pleasant subtle taste in an attempt to bring his thoughts back to reality.

'My doctor says it's all in my imagination and that it stems from the fear of loss I've had since Richard moved out.'

'Richard?'

'My husband. One day he just packed his bags and left, without even saying goodbye.'

Ivana had Leon's undivided attention again; she didn't even need to mention the direct parallels with Natalie's hasty departure.

'Do you know why he left?'

'It's this house. Albert von Boyten wanted to make some kind of artistic commune, open to friends and family who would be able to live here rent-free. That's the only reason why I, a penniless artist, was able to get this apartment in the first place. I could never have afforded the rent in this neighbourhood on two painting sales a month and my part-time job as a nurse. He even let me stay after we had ended our open relationship and I was no longer his muse.'

Leon pointed at the painting over the fire. 'Did you paint that?'

'Yes. When we were still in our wild phase. Albert had a lot of women, and I didn't mind. I don't know a single artist

113

who doesn't have a colourful sex life. And if not actively, then certainly in their head. Even Richard, a theatre director, who I met at one of Albert's parties, wasn't bothered by my relationship with Albert. For a while, after we moved in here together, we even had a *ménage à trois* going on.'

Ivana smiled in the same mischievous way as before, when she'd told Leon about her relationship with von Boyten.

'Clearly your benefactor had a soft spot for creative types,' said Leon.

'Oh yes. In his will he actually stipulated a quorum for artists to be granted apartments in the building.'

Leon nodded. That explained why Natalie and he had been approved.

'The house was supposed to be a creative oasis. But in the end it only brought him bad luck.'

She took off her glasses, which were slightly too large for her head, and chewed at the arms. 'Just like it has to all its tenants.'

Leon raised his eyebrows. 'What do you mean by that?'

'The pretty woman who used to live in your apartment, for example. She fell into the lift shaft and died. That set off an endless chain of tragic events.'

Leon nodded, thinking back to the cynical-sounding words of the building manager on the phone.

*The last tenant was blind. She couldn't even manage to operate the lift, let alone build a new entrance to her bedroom.*

'I'm no statistician, but over the years I've lived here now, an unusual number of tenants have died unnatural or at least premature deaths. Some committed suicide or were taken into psychiatric clinics – like Albert.'

'Von Boyten?'

She nodded. 'The biographies all say that Albert retreated to some unknown place in order to meditate, in keeping with his eccentric nature. It wasn't a voluntary exile, though, but a private psychiatric asylum. He died there some years ago, mentally deranged.'

'And his son inherited the house?'

'Exactly. But it didn't make him happy either.'

'What happened?'

Ivana hesitated. It looked as though she was wrangling with herself as to whether she was able to share this secret.

'No one knows exactly. His apartment was locked and shuttered from the inside. All his possessions – his money, clothes and documents – were still there. The only thing missing and which never appeared again was him. It was as though his own apartment had swallowed him up.'

*No wonder the building manager didn't want to put us in contact. It's not even possible.*

'Which apartment did Siegfried live in?' asked Leon, even though he was pretty sure he knew the answer.

'I really don't mean to scare you with my stories, Leon. But it was on the third floor, your apartment. As I said, I would have warned you against it had you come to me before signing the contract.'

Ivana craned her head upwards and gestured at the ceiling. 'Can you hear that?'

He shook his head, but then he heard the scales, much more muffled down here than in his apartment.

'Tareski will be the next one to lose his mind, I fear. He keeps practising the same piece over and over again. That's not normal, is it?'

Leon shrugged his shoulders. After everything he had experienced in the last few hours, he was certainly in no position to differentiate between normal and irrational behaviour.

'And then there's the Falconis on the first floor,' Ivana continued.

'What about them?'

'Have you ever noticed that the two of them are obsessed with keeping their door closed whenever someone walks by? And if you ring the bell they poke their heads out of the smallest gap possible, so you can't see in. I recently made the mistake of accepting some post for them, a heavy package that I carried downstairs all by myself. Do you think they thanked me?' Ivana Helsing stirred her tea energetically. 'They didn't even open the door. I was just expected to put the package down and disappear again.'

'That's strange.'

'Yes, isn't it just? I'd love to know what they have to hide. Sometimes I think . . . Oh, never mind.'

She waved her hand and gave an embarrassed smile.

'What?' asked Leon.

'It's not worth mentioning. I'm an old tattle-tale, anyway. Would you like some more tea?'

She reached for the pot.

'No, thank you very much, though.' Leon went to look at his watch and saw to his surprise that it was no longer on his wrist. While he was still thinking about whether he had taken it off or lost it, Natalie's phone beeped in his pocket, muffled by the blood-soaked blouse that he had stuffed into his overalls. The warning signal for the steadily dying battery acted like a wake-up call.

'Thank you very much for the tea, Frau Helsing, and sorry again for my rather abrupt entrance here, but I really must go now.'

'Of course, I understand,' said Ivana, a trace of melancholy in her voice, as though she didn't often have someone to talk to, let alone someone who actually listened. 'Please don't let me keep you.'

She accompanied him to the door, where she looked in amazement at the chain again, and Leon almost thought she was going to ask him why he hadn't realised he was in the wrong apartment as soon as he secured it. After all, a women's quilted jacket was hanging on the inside; but Ivana just said softly, 'Leon, could you do me a favour?'

'Yes?'

'You seem to be a good man. Don't make the same mistakes I did.'

'I'm not sure I follow.'

She glanced quickly through the spy hole, before adding quietly: 'This house is like a magnet. It holds on to you with all its might. And the longer you stay, the harder it is to get away.'

'Oh, I'm sure you don't really believe that,' said Leon, with a forced laugh.

'Only very few have the strength of will to get out. Like Richard. Like your wife.'

'You don't know anything about Natalie and me,' exclaimed Leon, a little more brusquely than he had intended.

Ivana opened the door and checked to see if anyone was in the stairwell. Then she whispered to him, with a conspiratorial look on her face: 'That may be true, but I'm too old to mince my words, so I'll be straight with you. Don't make the same mistake I did. Don't wait for her to come back – go after her.'

'You're saying I should move out?'

Ivana gave him a meaningful look. 'First the nightmares, then they come true, Leon. Get out of here while you still can. If you stay too long, the house will change you, and the evil in you will come out.'

She grabbed his hand and came so close that he could see the fine hairs on her top lip and feel her warm, stale breath on his face as she bid him farewell with this mysterious prophecy: 'First the nightmares, then the reality. Don't wait too long, otherwise you won't be able to fight it.'

117

# 22

As Leon climbed the steps to his apartment, he was thinking about what he needed to do not to lose his mind completely. But he didn't have much time to deliberate. As he went round the corner between floors in the stairwell, he heard someone calling out his name.

'Herr Nader?'

Leon looked up and took the last flight at a slower pace. The man standing in front of his apartment door had an intimidating look about him, and Leon wasn't sure if it was down to his bulky physique, the Gestapo-like coat or his self-assertive tone. As so often with men who were losing their hair, the age of the stranger was hard to guess, but he looked to be in an age bracket in which a receding hairline was no longer a disadvantage in the attraction stakes, certainly closer to forty than thirty.

'Leon Nader?'

'Yes, that's me,' answered Leon with a nod as he took the last step.

The stranger sighed in a way that could only be interpreted as *finally*, then pulled out his identification badge.

'Kroeger, Criminal Investigation Department,' he said, stretching out his hand. In the dim light of the hallway, Leon didn't have to worry about the policeman seeing how dirty his hands were, but he still felt sick with nerves. After all the inexplicable events, the last person he wanted around was a cop. He had just been thinking about calling Sven. He needed an ally, a friend at his side. Not someone whose job it was to uncover the darkest of secrets and pull them into the light of day to the disadvantage of their owner.

'Is something wrong?'

'Are you just coming home from work?' asked the policeman, as if he hadn't heard Leon's question.

'Yes … I mean, no.'

Leon brushed his sweaty hair from his forehead, then gestured at his overalls and worker's boots.

'I'm renovating,' he said, hoping this would explain his deranged appearance.

The policeman looked at him, his eyes containing a variety of green tones, reminiscent of camouflage fabric. Leon avoided his gaze.

'I tried to find you an hour ago, but you didn't answer the door. Your bell's broken.' As proof, Kroeger pressed the brass button next to the door, and he was right. No sound came from inside the apartment.

'I went out to get a bite to eat and decided to try my luck a second time.'

'Was that you knocking earlier?' asked Leon, remembering the sound he had heard when he was clambering down into the shaft. He regretted his unguarded observation at once.

'If you heard it, then why didn't you come to the door?' Kroeger looked him up and down with suspicion.

'I wasn't feeling well. I was on the toilet.'

The detective instinctively took a step back and wiped his hand on his coat, obviously regretting having shaken hands with someone who was potentially contagious.

'You do DIY while you're feeling unwell?'

'No, I . . . well, it came on quickly. I felt sick all of a sudden. That's why I stopped.'

'I see,' said Kroeger, although his face said that he didn't.

'What did you want to speak to me about?' asked Leon, trying to take back the upper hand in the conversation. He felt a little dazed again, as if he had been drinking, and his tongue seemed to get heavier with every word he said.

'I want to show you something,' declared the policeman.

*Show?*

'Perhaps it would be better if we could . . .'

'What?' Leon looked at the door as the detective jerked his chin towards it.

'Oh, right. Yes, of course.'

As he realised what Kroeger was getting at, he abruptly became aware of the next problem. 'I'm afraid I can't ask you in,' he said, patting his empty pockets under the policeman's suspicious gaze. 'I forgot my key.'

*Am I slurring?*

His own voice suddenly sounded foreign to him.

'You've locked yourself out?'

'Yes, I just wanted to fetch the post . . .'

Inside the apartment, the telephone began to ring.

'After you were in the bathroom and decided to stop renovating?'

'Yes,' confirmed Leon flatly.

The detective looked amused.

'Then it seems like today just isn't your day, huh?'

*You could put it like that . . .*

'Man, oh man. I think you really are a little out of sorts. Not only did you forget your key, but . . .'

The detective put his foot against the door, and the ringing from the telephone became louder.

'. . . you also forgot to lock up.'

120

The door opened with a creaking sound, although it could just as easily have come from Leon's throat.

'But that's impossible,' he exclaimed, making yet another blunder.

'Why?'

*Because I checked it was locked yesterday before going to bed, and have only left the apartment since then through my wardrobe.*

As they walked in, he heard his own voice coming from the answering machine in the hallway: '. . . reached the home of Natalie and Leon Nader. Please leave a message after the tone.'

A moment later they could hear the dulcet tones of a young woman speaking with exaggerated politeness on the tape: 'This is a message for Herr Nader from Geraldine Neuss at Bindner Jewellers. Please excuse the interruption during the holidays, but we just wanted to let you know your wedding ring is ready to be collected and hopefully won't be quite so tight any more.'

There were two beeps, then the connection was broken. Leon grasped the ring finger of his left hand, no longer feeling even the imprint on his skin. It had disappeared, along with any recollection of having taken the ring in to be adjusted.

'Are you OK?' asked Kroeger, and Leon realised he was standing there staring straight through the detective.

He was suddenly overcome by the urge to confide in somebody, and perhaps it wouldn't be so wrong to speak to a policeman, even if he would immediately become a suspect if he showed Kroeger the entrance to the tunnel system. Maybe Natalie had got lost in there and needed help? If that were the case, it would be negligent of him to hesitate too long purely out of fear of incriminating himself.

'Why don't we sit down in the living room?' suggested

121

Leon, unsure as to whether he should open the door to his bedroom in the man's presence.

What if he hadn't committed a crime after all? What if everything sorted itself out and Natalie came through the door laughing in the next moment?

*Oh, really? And what would she say? 'Sweetheart, did you find my mobile down in the shaft? I must have lost it when I tore off my thumbnail.'*

Leon shook his head, incapable of finding any explanation that would put his world back into place.

'Excuse me?' asked Kroeger, looking around the living room.

'I didn't say anything.'

'Yes, you did. You mumbled someone's name, I think.'

*Shit, now I don't even notice when I'm thinking out loud any more.*

'You must have misheard.'

'Hmmm.' The inspector nodded ponderously. 'I could have sworn you said "Natalie". Is your wife at home?'

'No.'

'Where can I reach her?'

Leon hesitated, then decided to tell the truth; it was already on record, after all.

'I have no idea. She hasn't come home for the last few days, that's why I called the police.'

'I wasn't aware of a missing person's report.'

'The officer said that with adults you have to wait at least fourteen days, unless there are unusual circumstances.'

Kroeger nodded again. 'That's correct. Otherwise we would waste all our time with marital crises.'

He stepped towards the mantelpiece and picked up a silver frame. 'This is a nice photo.'

'Yes. Natalie took that one.'

*On the day we met.*

'I only see pictures of you here,' said the detective in surprise. 'None of your wife.'

'Hazard of the job. Natalie is a photographer, she prefers to be behind the camera.'

'Hmm.'

Practically able to feel the policeman's mounting suspicion, Leon decided to find out the reason for his visit before saying anything else.

'What exactly did you want to show me?'

'This.'

Kroeger pulled a mobile phone from the pocket of his leather coat and handed it to Leon.

'Where did you get this?' asked Leon, immediately recognising it as his own. He wondered why he hadn't noticed it was missing.

'We seized it.'

*Seized it?*

'When?'

Kroeger posed an unexpected counter-question. 'Is everything OK with your eye, Herr Nader?'

'Sorry?'

'You keep blinking. And you're avoiding making eye contact.'

'I have nothing to hide,' lied Leon, changing the subject quickly by pointing at the phone. 'Where did you find it?'

'Given that it's part of a criminal investigation, I'm not able to say for investigatory reasons.'

*A criminal investigation?*

'Your contact details weren't saved, so it took a while before we were able to identify you as the owner via the network provider.'

*Investigatory reasons?*

Leon gripped the edge of the dining table. His nausea was growing by the second.

'Thank you for going to the trouble,' he murmured flatly. The phone lay in his hand like a foreign body. It had only 10 per cent charge left. As soon as he keyed in the pin code, a ringing sounded out. It wasn't coming from his hand, but the breast pocket of his overalls.

'You have another mobile?' asked Kroeger in confusion.

'What? Erm, yes.'

'Don't you want to answer it?'

'It's not important.' He shook his head.

He might be able to explain having Natalie's mobile in his possession, but if he pulled it out of his pocket together with the blood-soaked blouse, it would be another matter . . .

'Right then!' Kroeger was now stood next to him at the dining table, no longer interested in the frame on the mantelpiece. He waited for what seemed a painfully long time, until the phone had stopped ringing, before continuing.

'As I'm sure you can imagine, the police have better things to do than act as delivery boys. I'm not here to give you your phone back, but because we stumbled across some strange content while evaluating your saved data.'

'Content?'

'Pictures, to be precise. Open the photo gallery.'

Leon did as he was told, and the first image was like a stab to the heart. Casual acquaintances would hardly have recognised him and Natalie on the photograph, because they were both in disguise. He looked like an old man: with a walking stick, hunched back, a double chin and a red, alcoholic's nose. She was dressed as a beggar and also looked years older. Her masquerade was deceptively real; only her broad smile exposed her true identity.

'We took that at Halloween, just before leaving for a fancy dress party,' explained Leon.

Alongside her studies, Natalie had trained as a make-up artist, and that evening she had created a genuine masterpiece.

He thought back wistfully to the preparations. His favourite part had been the almost intimate caresses as she applied the make-up, the tender brush-strokes on the cheek, the stroking movements on the eyelids; her dark eyes and lightly parted mouth so close to his own lips.

'Lovely,' Kroeger said drily. 'But let's skip the first twenty snapshots. I'm not interested in how you spend your free time, but more in this.' The detective gave him the mobile back once he had scrolled down to the final pictures in the folder. Leon's eyes widened.

'That's private,' he said, his voice cracking.

'I know. But believe me, I wouldn't be here if it were merely a matter of your sexual preferences.'

The badly lit photo had been shot without the flash and showed Natalie sitting by the upholstered bed-head of their double bed. She was cross-legged, with her arms stretched wide above her head like someone bound to a cross, which in a way she was, for her wrists were in leather handcuffs, attached to the bed-posts with chains. She was wearing a man's vest ripped at the collar bone, which revealed more than it concealed, for her breasts were either wet or soaked with sweat. Either way, her erect nipples were plain to see despite the poor quality of the image.

Leon felt ashamed, a new feeling after all the worry, fear and panic he had suffered in the last hours. But the problem was not that Kroeger had trespassed into their intimate sphere and now knew about his wife's most secret sexual fantasies. The problem was that Leon had never seen this picture before. Nor all the others that Kroeger was about to show him.

At the behest of the policeman, he opened the next three images, each one worse than the last.

On the first, Natalie was completely naked, a rubber ball in her mouth. On the next, her eyes seemed about to pop

125

out of their sockets, so tight was the dog's collar around her neck. But the real shock came from the last photo in the unknown series, taken three days ago, at 3.04 in the morning.

*When I was sleeping . . .*

If it had been possible – with some effort – to interpret Natalie's facial expression as sexual arousal before, then on this her eyes were filled with raw pain. She was bleeding from her closed mouth, her right eye was swollen, and if Leon wasn't mistaken, her thumb was injured too.

'Is there something you can tell me about this?' asked Kroeger.

'Only that it has nothing to do with you.'

'We'll see about that.'

'What's that supposed to mean?' asked Leon, now certain he would not be showing this man the door to the labyrinth under any circumstances. Too great was his fear of finding out what he was capable of.

*What have I done to Natalie?*

'You can take whatever pictures you want,' said Kroeger. 'As far as I'm concerned you can hang from the ceiling fan by your knotted balls. As I've already mentioned, Herr Nader, the police aren't there to get mixed up in marital issues. But you don't need to be investigator of the month to figure out that something's not right here. Your wife disappeared shortly after these photographs were taken.'

Leon tapped his thumb on the now-dead mobile display and asked, 'Would I have phoned the police if I had done something that was against the law?'

Kroeger laughed throatily and turned to leave. 'You wouldn't believe how stupid most of the criminals we deal with are.'

Leon followed him into the hallway, becoming anxious when the policeman went in the wrong direction, towards the bedroom, the door of which stood ajar.

126

'This is the way out,' said Leon, a little too insistently. The detective stopped abruptly.

'Are you trying to get rid of me?'

'No. I just don't want you to go the wrong way.'

Kroeger looked Leon right in the eyes, frowning, then turned back.

'OK then . . .' he said in a threatening tone, reaching inside his coat. Leon felt sure Kroeger was about to pull out a pair of handcuffs or a weapon, but it was just a wallet.

'For the moment you seem to have a clean record, Herr Nader. So see my visit as a warning. As of now, we have the special circumstances we need to take your missing person's report seriously. And while we look for your wife, I'll be keeping an eye on you.'

He handed Leon his card.

'Please do yourself a favour, and call me as soon as you have something to say.'

# 23

'Sven? Where are you? If you get this message, please call me back as soon as you can. I need your help.' Leon cut the connection with his friend's voicemail and turned his landline phone over in his hands thoughtfully. Before him on the desk in his office lay the discoveries from the shaft: Natalie's blouse and mobile phone. The latter was charging before the battery died completely.

The police detective had taken Leon's mobile phone with him, saying that he wasn't yet able to release it on account of the fact that it was potentially evidence. Leon wasn't sure if that was legal, but he had only protested half-heartedly. An argument with Kroeger wouldn't have gained him anything, and would only have made the policeman more suspicious.

*Damn it, Sven. Why aren't you picking up?*

Normally his friend was always contactable, especially at times like these, when it was all or nothing in the final stages of a pitch.

Leon sat at the desk and reached for Natalie's phone. Since Kroeger left, he had already checked it. But with the exception of Dr Volwarth's contact details, he hadn't found any other entries, pictures or dates that seemed suspicious.

Many of the names in her contacts were, admittedly,

unknown to him, but that wasn't surprising given that Natalie had friends from her student days saved there, many of whom Leon hadn't met or only briefly, and to whose names he wouldn't have been able to put a face.

And yet he still had a strange feeling as he opened the list of missed calls and saw an unusually long number at the top.

*Who called Natalie while Kroeger was grilling me?*

Leon pressed to return the call. A large part of him wanted to hang up at the dial tone. But on the other hand, if someone on the other end had information about Natalie, he desperately wanted them to pick up.

It was a while before he heard a noisy ringing, which sounded like the dial tone of a foreign line.

'Hello?' Leon heard a man answer. The voice sounded tired, but despite some interference from what sounded a little like a vacuum cleaner in the background, it was clear and easy to make out.

'Hello?' asked Leon hesitantly.

'Yes, who am I speaking to?'

Recognising the voice now, Leon jumped up from his seat as though he had been electrocuted.

'Dr Volwarth?' he asked in bewilderment.

'Yes, speaking.'

Leon's first impulse was to hang up, but it was already too late for that, because the psychiatrist had recognised his voice too.

'Leon? Leon, is that you?'

'Yes,' croaked Leon after a brief pause, in which he tried in vain to collect his wits. 'Why are you, I mean, how . . .? I thought you were on your way to Tokyo?' he stammered.

'And that's exactly where you are reaching me right now. On my seat in the plane.'

'You've been flying for over twenty-four hours?'

'What's this about, Leon? Don't you watch the news? The snow closed all the airports and our departure was delayed until this morning.'

Leon went over to the window and pulled the curtains apart. It was dark outside in the courtyard, but he could see thick peaks of snow on top of the rubbish bins.

'How did you get this number?' Volwarth asked.

'I pressed redial.'

'But how? I didn't call you.'

'Not me, no. You called my wife.'

'What? No, that's not possible. I don't know your wife.'

'Oh no?' asked Leon, feeling rage surge within him. 'So why is your name in her contacts list? And why did you try to call Natalie exactly twelve minutes ago on her mobile?'

'Just a moment.' Volwarth now sounded as confused as Leon had at the beginning of their conversation. 'What did you say your wife's name was?'

'Natalie.'

'My God . . .'

'Why, what is it?'

After a brief pause, in which the background noise from the aeroplane cabin became louder, Leon was able to hear the muffled sounds of the psychiatrist moving in his seat, then Volwarth spoke in a quiet but urgent tone: 'Listen, that clears up a few things, Leon. But I have to end this call immediately.'

'What's *that* supposed to mean?'

'That I can't help you any further.'

'What? But you're my doctor. I confided in you that my wife has disappeared and that I'm scared I have something to do with it, that my illness might have come back. And now even the police think I'm violent, and they showed me these horrific pictures they found on my mobile. Shot in our bedroom, a place where a void opens up, literally. Dr

Volwarth, don't you think that, as my psychiatrist, you're duty-bound to help me in this situation?'

'Yes, you're right. And I wish I could.'

*Could?*

'Who the hell is stopping you?'

'Doctor–patient confidentiality.'

Leon choked as if Volwarth's last sentence had been forced down his throat. 'Just a moment, are you implying that Natalie is your patient too?'

'I really have to go now,' said the psychiatrist evasively, but Leon wasn't going to be shaken off that easily.

'What are you treating her for?'

'Please, I've already said too much.'

'She introduced herself with a different name, didn't she?'

'Leon . . .'

'I'd hazard a guess it was under Lené, her maiden name. Is that correct?'

'We're about to land, so we have to turn off all electronic devices. Goodbye.'

'You bastard!' bellowed Leon into the phone. 'What do you know about my wife? What's happened to her?'

'I have no idea what you're talking about, Leon. But it was really lovely to see you again after such a long time. Once again, congratulations on your wonderful apartment.'

*What's that supposed to mean?*

'I'm terrified that I'm losing my mind, and you spout this small talk? Please, Dr Volwarth, if you know something—'

'I just hope your fireplace starts working again soon, especially as it gets so cold over New Year.'

There was a crackle on the line, then the connection went dead.

# 24

Leon's rage had subsided, and a tense, all-consuming anxiety had won back the upper hand in his emotions.

He stood in the living room in front of the mantelpiece, in exactly the spot where the detective had stood searching in vain for photos of Natalie, and heard Volwarth's words replay in his mind: *I just hope your fireplace starts working again soon . . .*

Leon shook his head in a barely perceptible manner, like Ivana Helsing had done earlier while talking in her apartment. Then he kneeled on the protective brass fender in front of the fireplace. They hadn't used the open fire once since they moved in, because the chimney didn't work properly and there was a danger of carbon monoxide poisoning if they burned so much as a single log. It was an irritating problem that the building management had promised to deal with, but so far nothing had been done.

As a temporary measure, Leon and Natalie had installed a smoke-free ethanol heater. Artificial, plastic logs lay over a fuel chamber, creating an astonishingly genuine-looking and even warming light play.

'Our Las Vegas fireplace,' Natalie had joked. Like Leon, she tended to prefer more natural materials. 'Kitsch, but kind of cool.'

Thinking back to that day made Leon sad. Only a few weeks later, Natalie's laugh was just a memory of a time that was probably irrevocably lost.

*And now?*

After Volwarth had hung up, Leon had stood in his study as if nailed to the floor, wishing there were a lid on top of his skull so he could reach in and stop the carousel of his thoughts.

*How does Volwarth know the fire's not working?* was no longer the most burning question in his mind.

Only Natalie could have told him, but that was of marginal importance right now. Much more decisive was the fact that the psychiatrist had rudely ended their conversation with this very refrain, and there could be only one explanation for that.

*Volwarth wanted to give me a clue without damaging his professional integrity.*

'Come on, then,' said Leon to himself.

He removed the artificial pile of wood from the fireplace, then the pot with the fuel, and lit a match. The flame revealed the sooty, cracked inner wall of the fireplace, and as Leon poked his head into the opening, he couldn't help but think about the fairy tale of Hansel and Gretel, when the evil witch burns in her own oven after Gretel deviously lures her in there. His nerves were stretched to breaking point, and he looked behind him to make sure he was alone and that no one was standing there watching him.

*It has eyes, you know. The house, I mean.* He thought back to the cryptic words of the old Helsing woman, who was probably sat in front of her fireplace right this second, one storey down, talking to herself.

Once the first match had burned away between his fingers without him having seen anything, he lit another and tried to approach things in a more systematic way.

133

Thick, grimy soot – harking back to the days when tenants were lucky enough to have an intact chimney – covered his finger as Leon fumbled his hand around the base, centimetre by centimetre, in the hope of finding some hollow, groove or other feature that would suggest a hiding place.

Once he had checked the base and the walls of the fireplace, in vain, he moved to the chimney's smoke flap, which sealed the vent and, strangely, he couldn't open by hand.

Leon had to use the tongs to open it from the inside, and almost as soon as he had, after considerable effort, the obstruction that had been blocking the vent fell to the floor.

*What in God's name . . .?*

He flinched back from the small package as though it were a venomous snake. After a moment of shock, he bent over to pick up the object, which was wrapped in a plastic bag. It felt like a heavy book. Old, grey soot rose up towards him. Once he had taken off the wrapping, he realised that Dr Volwarth had led him to probably the most intimate document that Natalie had ever created.

Her diary wasn't very big, containing at most a hundred pages which had been bound into a rigid book. She'd only written on some of the pages, as Leon had established after wiping the soot from his fingers and sitting on a chair to inspect his find.

For the most part, the handwritten entries consisted of just one or two sentences, illustrated here and there with a drawing or photo.

Leon felt even more guilt than he had when searching Natalie's photography lab. By reading her diary entries, he was crossing yet another line, trespassing into forbidden territory.

*Should I leave him?* Natalie had asked her diary. The entry, made in her familiar, florid handwriting, was dated 28 February, just two months after they moved in.

134

I thought we were soul mates. But sometimes I don't even recognise him. It's almost as though he has two faces.

Leon's throat began to tighten and the tips of his fingers became numb. He flicked through a few insignificant entries about problems or successes in the gallery, and her father's approaching birthday – the fact that she didn't know what to buy him.

Then, at the beginning of June, he found a photograph. There could be no doubt as to what it meant, but Leon spent several tortured seconds trying to find another explanation to the one that was so obvious. But all his efforts were in vain.

The fact that he had never seen the ultrasound picture before was like a blow to the gut, and Natalie's entry made it even worse.

What should I do? I don't want to keep it. I CAN'T keep it.

'Tell me it isn't true,' said Leon, barely managing to get the words out. It felt like his throat had been sealed shut. He flicked further on, page by page, with every entry getting more nervous of finding the words he was expecting. Then he found them, dated two weeks later, just before the end of the first trimester.

Leon's eyes filled with tears.

The appointment in the clinic was awful. I only hope that Leon never discovers the truth.

'No!'

Something shattered inside him, something that would never be whole again.

'But why?' he whispered.

*We wanted that baby so much.*

At that moment he wished Dr Volwarth had kept his oath of confidentiality. He would never have wanted to find out this truth. He had been hoping the psychiatrist had some information that could have brought Natalie back. But now Leon felt further away from her than ever before.

*It was the right decision not to tell him. Things are getting worse and worse with him,* said an entry some weeks later. He felt just as agitated and shaky as Natalie's handwriting.

Her writing seemed rushed, fragile. No longer neat and artistic as he knew it to be from the notes she had so often left him on the fridge.

But that had been before, and *before* was clearly over.

*I'm afraid,* Natalie had written on one of the last pages, underlining the most terrible word in the sentence twice. *He's* hurting *me so much. It was all a terrible mistake. I have to leave him.*

'Our marriage? Me? The baby? Everything a mistake?'

Leon closed first the diary and then his eyes.

See nothing. Feel nothing. Forget everything.

'Am I responsible for what's happened to her?'

*From the abortion to her disappearance?*

Leon knew he was behaving oddly, sitting there having a conversation with the diary in his hand, but he couldn't help it.

'What did I do?'

Almost as soon as he had spoken the words out loud, he felt unbelievably tired, and this made him realise two things: firstly, he didn't have the strength for any more discoveries; he would lose his mind completely if he stayed in this apartment alone any longer, if in fact it hadn't happened already.

And he had asked the wrong question. The decisive factor was not what he had done in the past, but what he would do from now on that could damage himself or others.

*I can't go to sleep*, he thought, going into the bathroom to splash his face with cold water. *Not until I know the whole truth.*

He made a decision, the start of which entailed checking the front door to make sure he had secured it properly after Kroeger's departure. Normally he left the key in the lock when he was at home, but this time he took it out to keep on his person.

Leon knew how laughable these security precautions were in a building with doors hidden behind wardrobes, but he still checked the windows and searched every single room before sitting down in his living room and calling for help.

# 25

'Where the hell have you been hiding?' snarled Sven, his voice low and dangerous, as if he was only managing to hold back with a great deal of effort.

'I wanted to ask you exactly the same thing, I've tried to get hold of you several times already.'

'Well, you could have saved yourself the effort if you'd come to the party with me like we planned.'

By the fact that Sven spoke haltingly, Leon could tell how worked up his friend and business partner was. He had only heard him stutter this much once in recent times, and that was the day his mother had died.

'Which party?' asked Leon.

'Are you kidding me? Professor Adomeit? The executive director of the hospital consortium? The man with the sack of money and the golden fountain pen ready to sign our contract?'

*Oh Christ, the birthday celebration for Adomeit's fiftieth.*

Leon's hand rose to his forehead.

'I drove the four hundred kilometres to his holiday home out by the lake completely by myself.'

'I'm sorry, I totally forgot.'

'So I noticed,' said Sven, with a prolonged 'n'. Alongside 'd', this was the consonant that gave him the most difficulties.

'The idea with the tunnel connecting the hospital buildings was a hit, by the way!'

Leon closed his eyes. He had completely forgotten the fact that the model had disappeared from his study.

'Great, thank you. Why is it so quiet there?' asked Leon, who couldn't hear music, the clink of glasses, or any of the other usual sounds that accompany parties.

'Because I'm freezing my arse off on the veranda by the lake. It's too loud inside to take calls.'

As proof, Leon suddenly heard the rhythmic sound of the bass, as though someone had just opened the door to a club. Just as quickly, it stopped again.

'Where have you been? I tried your mobile a dozen times.'

'The police seized it.'

'What?'

Leon didn't know where to start. Ideally he would have liked to tell his friend about the door and the labyrinth, the thumbnail and the bloody blouse, but he couldn't do that on the telephone – and especially not while Sven was at a party.

Leon summarised the events of the last few days as briefly as he could, omitting the details that would cast doubt on his sanity.

Once he had finished, Sven's voice sounded even shakier than before, and Leon wasn't sure if it was exclusively down to the cold. 'So you're telling me your wife ran into the street in a distraught state, and you're scared you might have hurt her in some way?'

'Yes. And I'm afraid there's proof.'

'Sorry?' said Sven. 'The line is bad. What was the last thing you said?'

'There's proof.'

'The photos on your phone?'

'Not just that.'

'I'm not understanding any of this,' said Sven after a thoughtful pause.

*Believe me, neither am I.*

'Didn't you tell me during our last phone conversation that Natalie said she needed some space and that she was going to take some time for herself?'

'What? No, what gives you that idea?'

'Look, I'm not mad, you know,' protested Sven. 'You told me about the card she left you.'

'What card?'

'The one she pinned on your kitchen door before she went.'

All of a sudden Leon felt like his muscles had frozen. It took all of his strength of will to order his legs to carry him into the hallway.

'You must be mistaken,' he said to Sven, even though the proof was right in front of his eyes. Next to the newsletter from the building management, there was a postcard with an orange and yellow flower motif. Carefully, as though it might turn into dust, he freed it from the magnet and flipped it over.

*Dearest Leon*, began the brief note, composed by Natalie in her unmistakable handwriting. The postcard in his hand was shaking so much that he had trouble deciphering the lines that followed.

I need some space. I can't tell you any more than that,
I'm afraid, just that I need to take a few days to figure
out where we go from here. Don't worry. I'll be in touch
as soon as I'm strong enough.
    Your Natalie

No postage stamp, no watermark. And yet here it was. In his apartment. In his hands.

Without realising, Leon had let his hand holding the phone

fall to his side, and once he put the handset to his ear again he heard an engaged tone. Thinking he had lost the connection to Sven, he pressed redial, in the process answering a new incoming call.

'United Deliveries, Customer Service, good morning . . .'

'Who?' asked Leon, utterly confused.

'We would like to apologise for the inconvenience, Herr Nader.'

Leon was about to hang up on the woman with the impersonal sing-song voice, but then she said, 'We're very sorry, but for some reason your last order seems to have gone missing.'

Leon shook his head in frustration. 'I don't have time to talk right now. And besides, I received everything.'

'Really? Oh, then the mistake must lie with the delivery company. Because we don't have your confirmation of receipt.'

*No wonder with that idiot of a courier.*

Without saying goodbye, Leon switched back to the call with Sven.

'Are you still there?'

'Yes.'

The background atmosphere had changed now. His friend's voice sounded closer; presumably he was no longer outside and had managed to find a quiet spot in Adomeit's house after all.

'You're right . . .' Leon had gone back into the living room with the postcard and laid it on the dining table next to Natalie's diary. 'There really is a note from her.' He looked at the dappled sunflowers on the front. *Van Gogh. How appropriate. He was also an expert in madness.*

'But I can't remember how it got on to the kitchen door.' His voice started to crack. 'I can't remember so many of the things I do in my sleep.'

'Leon, I—'

'Please, let me finish.'

'No,' Sven cut in. 'Now it's time for you to listen to me, Leon.'

'OK.'

'You know I've never really warmed to Natalie. And I'm saying this to you now as a friend, even at the risk that I might not be one afterwards.'

'What?'

'I don't trust her. She's playing games with you.'

'What do you mean?'

'Just think about how rushed your wedding was. Why do you think she wanted everything to be so quick?'

'But *I* proposed to her.'

'Yes, but you always wanted to have a big wedding. She wanted it to be secretive and really small. Why?'

'That was down to both of us.'

'Really? And did you make a pre-nup in all the rush?'

'What do you mean? She's the one with the rich parents, I'm the charity case.'

'And what about our business, Leon? If we get this commission, it's only the beginning.'

'I don't understand what you're getting at.'

'I'm just listing the facts. You're the one who needs to put two and two together.'

'The facts are that something awful has happened to Natalie. *Before* she left me.'

'You mean the injuries?'

'Yes.'

'They looked terrible, right?'

'Yes.'

'As real as the make-up you guys put on for Halloween?'

Boom. Another blow to the gut.

'You're crazy, Sven,' said Leon listlessly.

142

'And you're looking at things from too one-sided a viewpoint. Who was it that told me so proudly that Natalie was a genius of transformation? Maybe she's deceiving you.'

'Sven . . .'

'No, trust me. You couldn't hurt a fly. I know you.'

'Perhaps not well enough,' Leon interjected, his voice louder. 'I'm holding a diary in my hands in which she wrote that I was hurting her. And that she was so afraid of me that she *didn't want to keep our child.*'

Beside himself with rage, he flung the book away. It somersaulted across the room, opening up into a 'V' shape and shedding some pages, before crashing into the wall near the door.

He regretted his outburst at once, but he couldn't take it back.

'I'm just trying to help you,' stuttered Sven as Leon bent down to pick up the pages from the parquet floor. There were two drawings and a photo, which he must have missed when going through the diary. He recognised the location in the snapshot, even though this picture was even more dark and shadowy than an ultrasound image.

With great effort, Leon was able to decipher the word, written in old-fashioned script above a picture of a lightning bolt.

DANGER

Before, he had thought he saw it at the end of a tunnel. But now he realised his mistake. The wall on which the warning sign hung wasn't a wall at all, but a door. And on the blurry photo in his hands, it was slightly ajar.

All at once Leon felt so exhausted that he needed to sit on the floor so as not to fall over.

'How long will it take you to get here?' he asked Sven,

who by that point had asked several times if his friend was still on the line.

'I've been drinking. I won't be able to leave until tomorrow morning.'

'Please hurry. I have to show you something.'

# 26

The second descent was even harder than the first, primarily due to the equipment Leon was carrying. This time he didn't want to be reliant on the sketchy background illumination of a mobile phone.

Nor did he want to venture into the labyrinth without protection, for fear that he really had escaped a genuine danger earlier and not just a stray cat. Leon had armed himself with a pocket torch and a crowbar, something that could be used as both a tool and a weapon.

Because he wanted to keep both hands free, he stowed most of it away in his tool belt, which he wore around his hips as he made his way down the ladder for the second time.

But, most importantly, he was now documenting every one of these steps with the head camera. He only hoped the radio signal would be strong enough to reach from the secret passageways of the labyrinth up to the laptop in the bedroom.

For now he was using the built-in miniature headlamp of the motion-activated camera as a light source. As he descended into the abandoned tunnel with this instrument strapped to his head, he didn't just look like a miner, he felt like one too. This time Leon avoided the falling hazard towards the bottom of the shaft by leaving out the loose rung.

Once at the bottom, he surveyed the remains of his first expedition into the unknown. The sight of the shattered torch on the floor was a warning not to test his luck again. He had escaped unscathed, albeit shell-shocked, the first time. But next time there might be more than just damage to his possessions.

'I'm now going to crawl through a low tunnel,' said Leon, in case the images were too dark for the camera.

He didn't want to leave any room for doubt if anyone looked at the proof later.

Once again Leon got down on all fours, and once again he crept head first through the roughly hewn stone shaft. Surprisingly, even the light didn't make it any easier.

A constrictive pressure descended on his chest, and he couldn't help but think of being buried alive; of people who, after some horrific mistake, wait for rescue and have to ration every breath until the oxygen supply eventually runs out.

*No one knows where you are. No one will look for you. Who knows if the passageways here are even stable?*

In his visions, he was trapped by stones and debris, his arms broken, with no chance of using the mobile phone.

Leon paused, held his breath and listened to his heart, which refused to settle and was making the pulse in his neck flutter. When he couldn't hold it any longer, he gasped greedily for air, air that smelled of dust, earth and his own sweat.

But not of clean washing . . .

That's what was missing!

Both the droning sound of the washing machine and the smell had vanished. Only the cold remained, but right now Leon was glad about that. His body was seething with tension, and he would use any way of cooling off he could find. Ideally he would have liked to take off his gloves, but he didn't want to risk injuring his hands.

'I'm just reaching a passageway,' said Leon, standing up. 'I'll call it the tube.'

Last time he had only been able to touch the rough walls, but now he saw that the tube was significantly shorter than he remembered.

Leon had almost reached the fork at the end when he felt a gust of air on his legs, carrying something with it that almost knocked him over. And yet it wasn't a physical object or living being, but a voice.

'Help! Please, I need help . . .'

'Natalie?' shouted Leon. He had recognised his wife's voice instantly, even though it was very faint.

A fleeting waft, no louder than a whisper underwater.

'Natalie, where are you?'

No answer. His call echoed into the labyrinth, the depths of which he didn't know and in which he was at risk of losing himself, in every sense of the word.

'Natalie, don't be afraid.' He was just about to add, *I'm coming to help you*, when he heard more voices.

A man and a woman. At very close proximity. He turned off the light on his headband and held his breath.

*Who is that?*

The voices, which seemed weirdly familiar, were coming closer.

*But from which direction?*

The woman's words were too faint to make out, but what he heard was enough to intensify his fear for Natalie.

*Are they coming from up ahead?*

'Damn it, not again,' he heard the man curse, and Leon turned in the darkness towards the voice.

*No, they're coming from behind. Or are they?*

147

'Why weren't you more careful? Hurry up. You have to get it out again somehow.'

There was a crashing sound, and Leon, who by spinning around had lost his bearings, stared into what seemed like a never-ending wall of impenetrable darkness.

He freed the crowbar from his tool belt and held it at head height like a club. Ready to strike.

As exhausted as he was nervous, he grabbed hold of his headband to activate the camera lamp once more. Then something blinded him so completely that he had to shut his eyes.

When he opened them again, a woman was standing right next to him, crying.

# 27

The shock penetrated Leon's whole body so intensely that he hit out instinctively.

Hard. With all his strength. Without thinking for even a second.

He hit the woman, who had her black hair pulled into a tight ponytail, right between the eyes. He wasn't able to swing far because of the low tunnel, but at least the tip of the crowbar must have ploughed deep into the bone of her skull.

Yet Frau Falconi stood there unmoving, before she spoke: 'Man, I'm not even sure if the damn thing is still in there.'

Staring at the cleft in her face, Leon felt like he was having an out-of-body experience. Then his neighbour from the first floor rolled her tear-filled, red-rimmed eye, the lid of which she was holding with both index fingers to stop herself blinking, and it dawned on him what must have happened.

Frau Falconi's head really was just an arm's length away from him, but she wasn't on his side of the passageway. She was on the other side of the wall! In front of her bathroom mirror!

'Can a contact lens just disappear behind the eye like that?' Leon heard her husband ask. His voice, like his wife's, was muffled.

Leon stretched his arm out and tentatively touched the splinter he had made in the panel on the wall with his crowbar. The glass was at head height, and was roughly as big as a flatscreen TV.

*A two-way mirror!*

From here Leon had a direct view into his neighbours' bathroom, while Frau Falconi could only see herself in the mirror, which on Leon's side must be strengthened with thick, soundproofed safety glass. His arm was sore from the impact of the crowbar jolting back into his bones. Frau Falconi, on the other hand, had heard and felt nothing, and continued the search for her lost contact lens unperturbed.

'No, the connective tissue stops them from going behind your eye and disappearing into your head,' she answered her husband, who had come into the bathroom.

Like his wife, his Italian roots were unmistakable: thick dark hair, brown eyes and healthy-looking tan skin even in winter. But in contrast to the well-groomed appearance of his wife, the husband was quite scruffy. While she wore a white, figure-hugging blouse, he had on a creased linen shirt hanging down over his pot belly. 'It's always the same with you. We need to talk about something important, and you start messing about.'

'Of course. I'm just poking my eyeball around specifically to annoy you.'

The couple's voices were coming from a small gap directly above the mirror, presumably connected to the bathroom's ventilation system.

Leon noticed a movement in the background, then saw the husband opening a bathroom cabinet and fetching out a brightly coloured sports bag.

'Our money's getting tight, darling.'

'You mean, *my* money.'

Herr Falconi pulled his face into a derogatory grimace behind her back.

'I saw that,' said his wife, without turning round.

Leon, who so far had been fixated on Frau Falconi's tear-stained face, took a step closer to the mirror to get a better look at the man. 'Will you be fetching some more soon?' he asked, fanning through the bundle of notes he had taken from the bag.

'That should be enough for now,' sighed Frau Falconi, who had taken a step away from the sink. Thanks to her fingers, her eye was now so bloodshot barely any white could be seen. Her nose was running too, but she made no move to blow it.

'For now, yes,' said the man, stuffing the money into the back pocket of his trousers.

'But if things carry on like this, soon we won't be able to afford the rent.' He made a fawning bow and feigned an apologetic expression. 'Sorry, I mean of course that *you* won't be able to pay the rent.'

'Let me worry about that,' said Frau Falconi, grabbing a tissue from the box on the basin. She was just about to blow her nose when she stopped abruptly and cocked her head to the side. It was a few moments before Leon heard what had caught her attention.

A soft melody.

*No, not a melody. Scales.*

Herr Tareski on the fourth floor had begun his piano practice again, and for some reason it was making Frau Falconi smile. She listened for a short while, as though enchanted, then followed her husband out of the bathroom. Leon didn't know what was bothering him more: that he had been plunged back into darkness, into a world between worlds that he understood less and less with every new discovery, or that, shortly before the light went out, he had the feeling Frau Falconi had given him a conspiratorial wink through the mirror.

151

# 28

An hour later Leon had switched sides. Now he was no longer standing in the tunnel, but in the bathroom; and it wasn't the Falconis', it was his own.

He took another swing, smashing the crowbar into the mirror again. But unlike down in the labyrinth, the glass here shattered, revealing a concrete wall.

No *two-way mirror. Logical.*

Leon laughed, close to hysteria.

*After all, why would you want to spy on yourself?*

And even if he did – was it plausible that he had constructed this world of shadows in his sleep: the wardrobe? The labyrinth? The mirror?

He wheezed, breathless from the fast climb and still exhausted from the fruitless attempts to open the door in the small passageway.

After the Falconis had disappeared, he remained in the darkness for a while, listening for further scraps of conversation. But he couldn't shake his confusion, numbed by the shock of realising that he could spy on his neighbours from down here. At some point (and he didn't know whether minutes or hours had passed) he turned the light on again and made his way to the DANGER sign.

The door was concealed so well that if he hadn't seen it

in black and white on the picture from Natalie's diary, he would never have found it in a thousand years.

Leon groped around the wall of the apparent dead-end, and didn't find anything to grab hold of. No gap. No edge. No hinge.

Secretly, he had suspected as much.

*After all the exertions so far, that would just have been too easy.*

He knocked against the wall looking for hollow spaces, hammered the crowbar against the sign, and even searched the surrounding walls and floor for hidden levers. But all in vain. Perhaps a blow-torch or sledgehammer would have come in useful, but against what?

And even if he did succeed in opening this secret door, would he really find Natalie behind it? Her calls had gone silent, just like Tareski's muffled piano playing, and by now Leon was no longer sure if he had even really heard her. He wasn't sure of any of his senses any more.

After the failed attempts to open the door, and feeling close to a mental breakdown, he had sunk down on to the earthy floor and buried his face in his hands.

Here, at the very lowest point of his despair, not knowing what nightmares lay ahead, he had the all-decisive thought: *Let's suppose I have a second, nocturnally active self. And let's assume that in my second consciousness I constructed a parallel world – then the entrance to this world can't be that complicated. Otherwise I wouldn't be able to master it in my sleep!*

Under this premise, everything argued against the idea that the door had to be opened with brute force.

Leon had pulled himself back to his feet and using his thumbs pressed with all his strength on the middle of the sign, as though it were the child-proof lock of a medicine container. At the same time he tried to turn the DANGER

153

sign clockwise with his other hand, something that presumably would have been much easier if he hadn't already bent the edges. But after the third attempt it made an audible click, then suddenly moved to the side.

That had been half an hour ago. Leon had gazed in amazement at the safety lock exposed behind the sign, touching it with his fingers and checking to see if any of the keys on his keychain fit. The euphoria he felt when his front-door key turned in the lock disintegrated as Leon discovered that he hadn't opened the door, just a postcard-sized cover, beneath which lay an electronic input screen. The buttons were inscribed not with numbers, but letters.

*Now what?*

He had the key but not the code.

Leon tried the first passwords that came to mind: *Natalie, Leon*, their surnames and pet names, and even *Morphet*. All without success.

Then his gaze fell on the inside of the lock's protection plate. On closer inspection, he was able to make out the thin pencil lines, which formed a series of letters. He read:

The violin is the key!

What was that supposed to mean?

*My sleepwalking self is making mnemonics I don't recognise in my conscious state!*

Leon had reached breaking point. Once again solving one mystery had only brought him another one, and now, standing before the ruins of his bathroom mirror, Leon became aware that he was neither physically nor psychologically able to figure this out alone.

He didn't want to wait any longer for Sven. No, he *couldn't* wait. He needed help.

*Immediate help.*

Leon hurried out of the bathroom into the hallway, picked up the telephone from the unit and took it into the bedroom. He had left Inspector Kroeger's card there, next to his laptop.

*What the hell?*

He stared at the keypad of his telephone.

The buttons lit up when pressed, and he could hear an electronic crackle when he put it against his ear and listened hard. But other than that, the line was dead.

*But I thought I charged it?*

No dial tone. Not even when he tapped in the first few digits.

*This can't be happening.*

He thought of Natalie's mobile, but couldn't remember where he had put it. Was it still down in the shaft? It wasn't in his pockets, and he couldn't see it anywhere else. So he went to the front door to go downstairs and ask Frau Helsing if he could use her landline, but then found himself confronted by the next problem. He was locked in.

Leon stared at his front door as though entranced, fixated on the lock, which normally contained a key. Then he remembered which lock he had left it in.

*Down there. In the labyrinth. Damn it . . .*

Leon let out a sigh that became a drawn-out yawn.

*I can't. Not again.*

But he didn't have a choice. He was unbelievably exhausted, his eyelids heavy as though they had weights hanging on them, yet it didn't matter. If he wanted to end all this insanity quickly, he had to go down there again.

*Into the labyrinth.*

But first he went to the bathroom to relieve himself, grateful for the destroyed mirror, which meant he could no longer see his reflection. If he looked only a fraction as bad as he felt, his appearance would scare even him.

While Leon stood there urinating, his gaze fell on the

155

medicine cabinet that Natalie had installed at head height over the toilet. Ever since the trip to Réunion, it had been well-stocked. Alongside aspirin, antibiotics, iodine, flu and diarrhoea remedies, pills for travel sickness, allergies and plasters, Leon also found the high-dosage caffeine tablets that she had taken in the initial phase of the gallery opening so she could work through the night. He swallowed two pills in one go and put the pack in his pocket.

*Just don't fall asleep.*

Then he readjusted the head camera, activated the lamp and armed himself a third time for his descent into the darkness.

# 29

Hours later, when Leon opened his eyes, he had no idea where he was.

He sat bolt upright in bed, startled awake by a sound like a squeaking tap. Seeing the make-up brushes on the bureau and the intact ceiling lamp above his head, he wondered why he felt so incredibly relieved.

He stroked his hand across the rumpled sheets, feeling the warmth from a body that must have been lying next to him until moments ago. And then he smelled it: the perfume, that subtle summery scent he had missed so much in his nightmare.

'Natalie?' he called, his voice still thick with sleep.

'Yes, darling?' he heard her answer from the neighbouring room.

Calm, relaxed, cheerful.

*Thank God.*

The incubus the nightmare had left behind began to lose its intensity.

*It was all just in my imagination!*

'You won't believe the crazy dream I had,' he called, starting to laugh.

He looked at the wardrobe, which was in its familiar place. In the light of day, it looked much too heavy to be moved without help.

*There's no door. No shaft. No transparent mirror.*

'I dreamed I discovered a labyrinth behind our bedroom wall while I was sleepwalking,' he said, shaking his head in disbelief at his own words. He made sure there was no USB stick in the laptop on the bureau, then jumped out of bed. He felt well rested and motivated for the first time in ages.

'There were passageways down there, and mirrors through which we could spy on the Falconis. Can you imagine? It was a nightmare, and I was afraid of falling asleep.' Leon heard the toilet being flushed in the bathroom.

'And I filmed myself, like that time when I was a kid. Can you hear me, Natalie?'

'Loud and clear, darling.'

The rushing sound from a tap being turned on swallowed his wife's words.

'It was like in a computer game, completely insane. You had disappeared, and I found all these clues everywhere that led me to a different level or to a new door I needed to look behind. But do you know what the strangest thing was?'

'No, what?'

Leon wrapped his hands around his upper body, shivering. He was naked and, like always, Natalie had turned down the heating before going to bed.

'I can remember all of it, every detail. Normally I forget my dreams as soon as I wake up, but this time I can even remember what I was thinking just beforehand.'

Leon opened the door of the wardrobe to get some clothes out.

*My last thought down there, before I fell asleep in front of the secret door with the* DANGER *sign, was:* You have to stay awake. Get your front door key, climb back up, fetch help. But for God's sake don't fall asleep.

'I was so scared of what I was capable of while sleep-

158

walking that I wanted to stay awake at all costs. I even took some of your Hello Awake pills from the medicine cabinet.'

'I know,' said Natalie, with a voice that was no longer coming from the bathroom.

Leon clapped his hand over his mouth in shock.

'You just wanted to get your key from the DANGER door, but you suddenly felt so tired you fell asleep right there with the camera on your head, is that right?'

*No, please no. Don't let it start all over again.*

His wife's voice sounded so clear, as if she was standing right in front of him. But there was nothing there but . . .

. . . *the wardrobe!*

'Natalie?'

Leon pushed the hangers to the side, as if he genuinely believed his wife could be hiding among the clothes like a child.

'Darling, where are you?'

'Here, I'm here.'

'Where's HERE?'

'I don't know. It's so dark. Please help me!' said Natalie in a voice that sounded more distant now, but its source hadn't changed. It was still coming from right behind the wardrobe.

*But that's impossible.*

Leon tore out the whole clothing rail, hangers and clothes included. Then he kicked the rear panel until it gave way and fell to the side.

Instead of the vault door that Leon was expecting, he found himself staring at a recently bricked-up section in the wall. The mortar between the bricks was still damp; Leon was able to leave fingerprints behind in the grey sludge.

'Get me out of here,' Natalie pleaded, close to tears now.

Her pleading was like a downpour of icy water. Leon

took a step back, stumbling over the crowbar that he had used to hit the mirror earlier.

*But EARLIER was a dream. And NOW is reality, isn't it?*

'Leon. Get me out of here before it's too late!'

Natalie's despair was like a baby's crying: impossible to ignore. Guided by his primal instincts, Leon grabbed the crowbar and started raking out the mortar.

'I'm coming,' were the last words he uttered before he managed to get some purchase between the bricks. Quickly, much too quickly, the first small crumbs of brick began to come away from the wall, then shards, then finally a whole brick.

'Hurry. Before you fall asleep again,' he heard Natalie call, and then came the water.

A dark drop bulged out, then it began to gush as though a valve had burst, and before Leon had time to press his hand against the hole in the wall, a fountain shot out. There was so much pressure that more and more bricks broke free, until eventually the entire wall collapsed over Leon.

He tried to scream, but only breathed in cold, dirty-tasting water, which he couldn't cough up because the pressure on his chest was growing and growing. Something pulled him down into the depths, threatening to drown him in its wet embrace.

Leon hit out, thrashing his arms and legs, realised he was trapped by something, then pushed himself against it with all his strength and finally managed to break through a viscous upper layer with his head. He opened his eyes wide, gasped for air and coughed. And with his attempts to purge the liquid from his windpipe, the dream ended.

# 30

Leon soon wished he was still in the sleep paralysis from which he had just freed himself.

At least then he wouldn't be lying fully clothed in his bathtub, covered with some liquid that smelled like iron, and a distant hum in his ear, not knowing whether the red stains came from one of his wounds or from the other, motionless creature that was in the bath with him.

*What IS that?*

He had touched it with his hand, and felt intense disgust as his fingers sank into the soft body under the water. He had gone through all the harmless explanations in his mind: a sponge, a flannel, a toy, but he couldn't fool himself. The fur had belonged to a living thing once, as had the tubular internal organs that were floating on the surface of the water.

Retching, Leon jumped out of the water, and in the process became entangled in the entrails, unintentionally pulling the animal over the edge of the bathtub.

*Alba?*

The dead cat thudded on to the tiles with a dull splat, its lifeless eyes fixed on Leon, the mouth open in a final hiss that seemed to have got stuck in its throat.

Leon, too, opened his mouth, because he had become so nauseated he could no longer breathe through his nose.

The smell of blood was just as intense as the sound of hammering on wood that had been coming from the hallway for a while now. It wasn't the only way that someone was trying to make their presence known at the front door. The impatient visitor was also ringing the doorbell, and it was reverberating through the whole apartment.

*I thought it was broken?* Leon asked himself, as close to hysteria as to a mental breakdown.

*My wife has left me because I've mistreated her; I can no longer tell the difference between dream and reality; I wake up in the bathtub with a dead cat – and now I'm worried about the doorbell?*

He shuffled out of the bathroom and crept along the corridor like a burglar: slowly, carefully, taking care not to make a sound. This was practically impossible, as his soaking boots squelched with every step. On top of that, he was struggling not to lose the left boot, which for some reason was missing its lace.

There was still water in his windpipe, and Leon had to cough. But there was no danger of the person at the door hearing him, given the din they were making already.

*Who the hell is it?*

Leon looked through the peephole and closed his eyes in relief.

'Thank God,' he said, close to tears with happiness.

The knocking and ringing died away.

'Leon?' asked Sven through the door.

'Yes.'

'What are you playing at? Open up, will you!'

'Just a second.'

Leon patted his pockets and was astonished to feel the bundle of keys that he thought he had left in the lock of the DANGER door in the labyrinth.

*How did they get back in my pocket?*

162

It was a struggle to get the key out of his damp pocket, before he opened the door to his friend, who pushed past him into the apartment, gesticulating wildly.

'Leon, I've been outside your door for a quarter of an hour already, and . . . Oh God.' Every trace of rage disappeared from Sven's face as soon as he looked at Leon.

'What in God's name happened to you?' he asked. At least, that's what Leon presumed Sven *wanted* to ask, because his stuttering was worse than it had been in a long time.

'I'm so glad you're here,' said Leon, turning towards the mirror. Then he understood why Sven was looking at him in such shock. He was still wearing his overalls, but now they were black from being drenched with water, or perhaps because of the blood, and that was not the worst thing about his appearance by far. His face looked as though he had made himself up like a clown and then put his head underwater: black and red make-up was daubed across his forehead and cheeks, down to his chin. Soot-like dirt made his hair stick together in thick strands, standing up erratically or clinging to his skull like algae. His red, inflamed eyes, over deep bags, completed the look of someone who was severely ill, with the worst symptoms still to come.

'I need your help,' croaked Leon, whose voice had failed at the sight of himself.

'Are you having a breakdown?' asked Sven, trying to form short sentences.

'No, it's not the work.' Leon giggled, because the question seemed so absurd to him. 'I haven't done any work since the model disappeared.'

'Disappeared?' Sven stared at him with an expression of rising disbelief.

'Yes. Gone. No longer there. Like Natalie. I told you. I think our work is down there with her in the labyrinth.'

'Where?'

'In the labyrinth I discovered behind my wardrobe. Come on, I'll show you the door.'

Leon grabbed for Sven's hand, but he pulled away just before their fingers touched.

'You have a fever!'

'No. Yes, possibly. I'm not sure.'

Leon searched in desperation for the right words to explain to Sven the insanity he was imprisoned in. When he didn't find them, he pressed his fists against his temples in despair. 'I don't know what's happening to me. Please, I'm begging you. Let me show you the door.'

For a few moments they stood silently before one another, then Sven nodded hesitantly and sighed. 'OK.'

Leon was relieved. 'Thank you. Really, thank you. Come with me.'

He turned round after every two steps to make sure Sven was really following him. 'Here it is,' he said, once they had entered the bedroom.

'Where?'

'Here . . .'

Leon positioned himself by the side of the wardrobe and braced both hands against it, like a runner stretching his muscles before exercise.

'I just need to push the thing to the side so that—'

Leon stopped in bewilderment. Even though he was pushing with all his strength, the wardrobe refused to budge by even a millimetre.

'Help me?' he asked, but Sven just lifted his hands dismissively.

'I've seen enough.'

His gaze wandered over the chaos Leon had left behind in his bedroom during the last few days: clothes lay strewn wildly, the metal chair in front of the bureau was on its side, the glass shards of the ceiling lamp lay among the crowbar and other work tools from the upended toolbox.

'I think you must be really burned out,' said Sven with a stutter, eyeing the trainers with the melted soles by his feet warily. They lay next to a pair of used latex gloves.

'No,' retorted Leon, more loudly than he had intended. 'It's worse than that. Believe me.'

*I can't let him leave again. Not before I've proved it to him.*

Leon had let go of the wardrobe and was now down on his knees, peering under the bed.

'What are you looking for?'

'My headband. My head camera. I filmed it all while I was down there.' Leon sat up and gave a tortured grin. 'Of course, God, I'm so stupid. You can see it all yourself. Come on.'

He jumped up and went over to the laptop on the bureau, which was still turned on, but in energy-saving mode.

'Wait, soon you'll understand what I'm talking about . . .' Leon pressed the escape button multiple times. As the screen came back to life, he turned – and found himself alone in the room.

'Sven?'

*No, please no. Don't let him have disappeared too.*

He rushed into the hallway, looking frantically in all directions.

'Sven?'

Instead of an answer, he heard the creak of the parquet floor, relatively close by in the stairwell.

'Sven, come back!' he called after his friend, running towards the exit. Rushing to catch Sven at the lift, Leon almost stumbled over him, as he didn't reckon on Sven being ducked down directly behind the front door.

'Hey, watch out. Otherwise you'll break it!'

'Break what?' asked Leon breathlessly. Instead of answering, Sven stepped to the side.

165

'*Voila!* Our vanished model,' grinned Sven, who was speaking more easily now. He lifted up the cardboard model of the hospital renovation with both hands and carried it past Leon.

'But, but, but, but . . .' Now it was Leon's turn to stutter. 'But that can't be possible.'

'And why not?' asked Sven on his way into the study.

'Where did you get it from?'

Sven had reached the desk and was placing the model in the middle of the work surface. 'Where do you think? I picked it up, remember?' Worry lines appeared on his forehead. 'You haven't forgotten that, have you?'

'Yes,' sighed Leon.

*Like so many things.*

'I guess I must have been sleepwalking when you came.'

His friend gave him a mocking look.

'Don't be ridiculous. That's impossible. I had a long conversation with you.'

'Well, that can happen in an unconscious state too.'

'You're kidding, right?'

'No. It's unusual, but not all that rare for sleepwalkers to act almost like normal, conscious people,' explained Leon in agitation. As he spoke, his thoughts were crashing together in his mind.

*Who knows how often I fall asleep? And if I don't always have the camera on? What else have I done in my sleep that isn't on the tapes?*

'Some cook meals for themselves, and by the next morning they've forgotten that they ate a salami pizza in deep sleep and washed up the dishes afterwards,' he continued. 'Others have whole conversations with their partners, go for a walk, turn the TV on or start up their cars.'

*And others enter into a gruesome underworld in order to hurt their wives . . .*

166

Leon didn't want to dwell on this last thought.

'There is a simpler answer to all this, partner,' said Sven as he walked out of the study. 'You're just overworked.'

Leon sighed. 'No. That's not it. I wish it was, but it's not. You have no idea. You don't know what's happening here . . . what happens to *me* when I sleep. I filmed it. Please believe me. Watch the tape.'

Sven groaned, and he sounded almost amused. 'A film?'

'Yes.'

'Of you sleeping?'

'Exactly.'

'And it's on your laptop?'

'In the bedroom. Please.'

For a while the friends didn't say another word, then Sven rolled his eyes like a father who couldn't say no to his son's ridiculous request.

'Fine. But first I need to use your bathroom.'

'What?'

'The toilet. I need to go.'

'No.'

Leon made a step to block his way, but it was too late. His friend had already opened the bathroom door.

'What the . . . Oh God!'

Sven flinched as though he had just been lashed in the face with a whip.

'You're sick,' he whispered. Strangely, when he lowered his voice, the stutter disappeared.

'That wasn't me,' said Leon, pointing at the dead cat on the tiles.

'I mean, it wasn't *the* Leon that *you* know.'

'Get away from me,' exclaimed Sven with a look of disgust on his face, stretching both his arms out to keep Leon at a distance.

'No, you have to stay!'

167

Leon screamed so loudly that spittle flew from his mouth. He grabbed Sven with both arms to keep him from going by force if necessary, but he was too weak. Sven had no difficulty in freeing himself from his grasp.

'Don't touch me!' he panted, backing towards the exit with his hands balled into fists.

'Please, Sven. I filmed everything. Myself, the shaft, the tunnel. Even the Falconis behind the mirror.'

He begged Sven to stay, to look at the video, but his words just drove his friend from the apartment more quickly.

'You've completely lost your mind,' shouted Sven. These were his last words as he flung open the front door and disappeared from view. Leon could only hear his heavy footsteps hammering down the stairs.

*And now? What do I do now?*

Leon would have hurried after him, but just the memory of Natalie fleeing into the stairwell only a few days ago under similarly mysterious circumstances – perhaps to disappear from his life for ever – held him back.

He leaned against the door from the inside, exhausted, closing it with his back and beginning to talk to himself again.

'I should get out of here. Ivana was right. It's the building. I have to get out of here.'

He went over to the telephone table and picked up the landline from its unit.

'I have to get out of here.'

When he heard the dial tone, he lost it completely. Leon laughed so hard that his whole body shook.

*My key. The model. The dial tone – they're all back.*

'Only my sanity is still nowhere to be found.'

Giggling hysterically, he went back into the bedroom to fetch the policeman's card. It was next to the laptop, and at least his memory didn't fail him on that point.

'Hello, Herr Kroeger? Please come and pick me up,' he laughed breathlessly as he dialled the inspector's number. After the fourth digit, he heard an engaged tone and stopped in confusion.

Clearly the blinking light of the USB stick in the laptop had distracted him so much that he had delayed too long dialling the number, and now needed to start again from scratch.

'No. Things can't go on like this,' he said to himself. 'I don't want to see what I recorded.'

*During my last sleep phase. After I fell asleep in the tunnel in front of the* DANGER *door.*

'I don't want to see it,' repeated Leon in a whisper.

*Not while I'm alone,* he added in his head.

But then he leaned over to lift up the metal chair and put it in front of the laptop screen.

# 31

A few minutes later Leon ran back into the bathroom so quickly he almost lost his boot that was missing its lace.

*Too late. Damn it. Hopefully I won't be too late.*

His wet clothes rubbed against his skin with every movement, but right now that was the least of his worries.

*I shouldn't have watched it*, he thought, cursing himself mentally. But how could he have resisted the blinking light when it might have signalled the solution to all his problems?

His hopes had been dashed, of course. Even worse than that: the images on the last recording had punished him ruthlessly for his lack of self-control.

If he had interpreted the video correctly, he had much bigger problems than he'd feared. Of the huge volume of material that had now been collected by the hard drive, he had watched only the very last, continuous recording, the first seconds of which were entirely unspectacular: the video had predominantly shown walls, stones and steps, in other words the path that Leon had walked along – from the door with the DANGER sign, out of the shaft and back to his apartment – almost as soon as he had fallen asleep.

*The violin is the key!*

Leon had been expecting to see himself operate the keypad and open the secret door.

*But instead, I did something much worse.*

He hadn't even glanced at the secret door at the far end of the dead-end tunnel, but instead went straight back, clambered up into his apartment, and pushed the wardrobe back in front of the opening in the wall. Still sleepwalking, he had then hobbled into the bathroom with strangely wooden movements.

At this point the bathtub wasn't yet filled with bloody water, Alba wasn't yet lying dead on the tiles, and apart from the debris from the destroyed mirror, there was no sign at all of the chaos Leon would unleash in just a few minutes.

Right now Leon was stood exactly on the spot where he had stopped and stared at the ceiling in the video.

*Literally.*

Directly above the toilet, a cover panel had slipped to the side, which until now he had always assumed was the casing for the service box of the water thermostat.

*Not the first mistake he had made since moving in.*

He clambered on to the toilet lid, on which his boots had already left prints, and pushed against the cover above his head. In his hurry he had left the torch in the bedroom, but the bathroom light was enough to illuminate the start of the chimney-like shaft and the rungs leading upwards.

Everything was exactly as he had seen it on the video, with one exception: the piano playing had stopped. While before he had been able to hear the soft but unmistakable sounds of Tareski's scale practice on the film's audio, now nothing but silence came out of the newly discovered exit.

*A deathly silence*, he thought as he grabbed the first rung above him.

He was tired and weak, and no wonder, for it seemed he had spent the last few hours doing anything but sleeping. The cold, hard edge of the rung didn't trigger his memory

171

as he grabbed it, nor did the musty smell of mould as he struggled his way upwards, but such recollections would have been highly unusual anyway.

Like most sleepwalkers, Leon couldn't remember his nocturnal activities. For that reason he wasn't surprised that the narrow shaft, which was becoming darker over his head by the second, seemed so unfamiliar.

*Quickly. Hurry. Don't lose any time.* He drove himself on in his head.

Halfway, shortly before the light shining up from below threatened to be extinguished, plunging the bricked walls into darkness, the fingers of his right hand unexpectedly touched a scrap of material.

Leon groped around his knee and found the corresponding rip in his trousers. So far he hadn't noticed that he must have caught his right leg on a sharp edge of the ladder in his sleep. But ruined clothing was the least of his worries; right now it was a matter of life and death.

*What have I done?*

Unlike when he ended up in Ivana Helsing's apartment, this shaft didn't lead into a bathroom, but a small chamber. The windowless room into which Leon had crept – through an already open floor panel – was in complete darkness, so he could hardly see his hand in front of his face. From the video recording, he knew the room had a square layout and was utterly empty.

Crawling on all fours, he groped around the wooden floor until he found the head camera. He had clearly lost it on his way back.

Leon switched on the camera's lamp and shone it at the path to the door.

He knew he had to go to the right. And he knew he didn't need to be quiet. Tareski wouldn't wake up even if a bomb went off in his apartment.

Leon hung the headband of the camera around his neck and ran along the corridor, flinging the door to the living room open.

'No!' he screamed, as he met the sight before him.

It had looked unreal on the video; not as gruesome, more like an illusion that could be erased simply by deleting the recording. But Tareski's bulging eyes, his foaming mouth and bloated, blue-violet face could not be made to disappear at the touch of a button. The sight of the chemist lying lifelessly in front of his piano on the carpet would haunt Leon for the rest of his life, he was sure of that.

He looked around and noticed a pair of scissors on a side table near the window. He reached out for them, even though they probably wouldn't be of much use now.

On the recording he had crept up behind Tareski as he sat there unsuspectingly at his piano. The chemist's eyes had been closed in concentration, as could be seen in the reflection of the polished, black lacquered surface of the piano. Somewhere between the chamber and the living room, Leon must have loosened his shoelace. A few steps later he had lurched forward swiftly and wrapped it around his victim's neck.

Tareski had gasped for air. His eyes, now dull and lifeless, had been wide open. In reaction he had tried to get his fingers under the noose Leon was using to choke off his air supply. At the same time he had reared up, forcing them away from the piano bench, and tried to turn to see his treacherous attacker, but when he couldn't he concentrated on mere survival, directing all his efforts towards finding a way to breathe again.

At some point, after Leon had tied a knot in the lace and left Tareski to choke in front of his piano, the chemist had managed to get a thumb under the noose. Clearly Leon had only tightened it half-heartedly or – which would be even worse – intentionally left a little leeway so the death throes lasted longer.

'I strangled him,' whispered Leon in devastation, kneeling. Tears rolled down his face, and he felt such intense guilt that for the first time he understood why people took their own lives. He put the scissors at the knot, accidentally knicking Tareski's skin. And it was lucky he did, for otherwise there would have been no pain reflex. Tareski's upper lip trembled slightly, but it was still a sign of life.

Without wasting time feeling for a pulse, Leon began to resuscitate Tareski. He turned the chemist on to his back, applied both hands in pressure-point massage above the heart, and . . .

Three . . . two . . . one.

*Nothing!*

'Come on!' he shouted, starting over again.

Three . . . two . . . one.

Leon flexed Tareski's neck and pressed his lips on to the chemist's open mouth. Fired by the hope that it might not be too late after all, he expelled the air from his lungs into Tareski's; felt how his upper body swelled and sank down again.

'Come on. Please . . .'

Leon switched back to heart massage, feeling like all his movements were in slow motion. Whenever he rammed down on Tareski's ribs, thoughts shot into his mind like lightning bolts.

Three . . .

*It's not just about Natalie. Or Tareski. I'm connected to all the apartments, I can spy on all the neighbours.*

Two . . .

*I'm a fan of the architect's work, I studied von Boyten.*

One . . .

*We didn't choose this apartment. It chose us.*

Zero.

At the end of the fourth interval, Leon was physically forced backwards. Tareski reared up beneath him, vomiting and wheezing at the same time. And then came the spasms.

*Thank God!*

Tareski's distorted body shook in a vicious fit of coughing. Leon feared the brought-back-to-life chemist still wasn't getting enough oxygen. Then, between two convulsive attacks, Tareski managed to suck in a stream of air, and the whistling breaths accompanying it were like music to Leon's ears.

'I'm sorry,' said Leon, knowing how inadequate the apology was for what he had done, even if he had been in a state in which he wasn't criminally responsible. Even if his attack hadn't caused any lasting physical damage – from this day on his neighbour would never feel safe again. Not when he went for a walk in the evening. Not when he sat in his car and looked in the rear-view mirror. And certainly not in his apartment, where he had been attacked completely out of the blue.

'I'll fetch help,' said Leon, pretty sure he wasn't getting through to Tareski at all. The poor man may not be fighting for his life any more, but he was still struggling for air, incapable of registering anything. Perhaps he could taste the blood in his mouth from his chewed-up tongue, possibly he could hear his own choking and wheezing, maybe the epileptic pumping of his heart and the blood crashing against his eardrums with the force of a water cannon. But certainly Tareski didn't hear the sound that cut Leon to the quick as he was looking around for a telephone.

*That's impossible.*

Leon turned back to the piano, in front of which the chemist was still cowering in an embryonic posture. He stared at the keys, before which sat no one but which were

175

still moving regardless – creating exactly the notes he had heard so often in the past few months.

*But how . . .?*

Leon took a step closer and saw the thin cable concealed on the side of the piano and running past his feet, presumably to a power point in the wall.

Bewildered, he looked between the chemist and the electric piano, which had clearly been programmed. The rhythm of the scales was halting and sounded unpractised, and now and again, seemingly by coincidence, there was a discord, as if someone had played a wrong note.

*But none of this makes any sense.*

Leon leaned over the keys, studying the open sheet music, then looked at Tareski, who by now had struggled up on to all fours and was coughing like a dog – and at that moment he realised, with painful clarity, the code that would open the secret door in the labyrinth.

# 32

Going back to the labyrinth through Tareski's chamber wasn't an option.

Leon wanted to return, which theoretically would have been possible as soon as he got back to his own apartment. But the secret door in his bedroom was blocked to him now that he could no longer move the wardrobe. This was probably due to the depth of Leon's exhaustion, and his dwindling strength. He would fall asleep again in a matter of seconds if he allowed himself even a moment's rest – but then again his inability to move the wardrobe was just as inexplicable as everything else that had happened to him so far on his search for Natalie, a search that was increasingly becoming a search for himself.

Either way, the consequence remained the same: if he wanted to test his suspicion, Leon would have to choose another entrance to the world between the apartments. And for that, only one possibility remained.

He unlocked the chemist's front door. Tareski was still the worse for wear, but significantly better than before. By now he had managed to get himself on to the couch and wasn't coughing as loudly. Leon didn't know whether his neighbour had recognised him or not, but right now he didn't care.

All that mattered was getting back to the DANGER door in the labyrinth as quickly as possible.

In the stairwell, Leon was met by a dull hammering and the screeching of a chainsaw, which immediately swallowed up the mysterious scales of the piano.

The scent of fresh woodchips hung in the air. Judging by the noise level, the builders were on the ground floor.

*My God, has that much time really passed already?*

Leon thought back to the notice from the building management. When he last looked at the magnetic board on the kitchen door, the renovation work had still been three days away. And now the workers were here, tearing up the floorboards on the steps.

He wanted to take the lift, but it was stuck on the ground floor, presumably blocked by the builders (*Be prepared for long waits!*). Leon had no patience, so he took the stairs.

Luckily for him, the works on the stairs had not progressed very far, so he was able to get to the second floor unobstructed, where he smoothed his hair with the palm of his hand and a little spit before ringing on the front door.

The din on the ground floor was so loud that he couldn't hear any sounds coming from inside the apartment. Impatient, he dispensed with all politeness and rang the bell repeatedly, until eventually the door edged open and a bony foot appeared in the gap.

'Herr Nader?' asked Ivana Helsing in surprise, once she had managed to open the door fully. She hadn't been able to use her hands, because she was holding a pile of small packages covering the expanse from her belly button to her chin.

'I wasn't expecting you,' she said, bending awkwardly to balance her load on a chair next to the bureau. 'I thought you were the delivery boy I arranged for a pick-up.'

Ivana didn't seem disturbed by Leon's appearance. Even the head camera flapping around his neck failed to draw a reaction. She was a little dishevelled herself, and looked considerably older than during their last encounter. The shadows under her eyes were darker, her skin greyer, and her hair was sticking up at odd angles from her head as if he had woken her.

'eBay,' she said and grinned impishly, glancing at the packages. 'You don't want to know what some people with strange fetishes order from old people like me. Well, you're married to an artist, so I'm sure you're not unfamiliar with such things. And these little packages help me to enjoy my retirement more.'

'Sure,' answered Leon absent-mindedly, not even listening properly to what Ivana was saying. He was distracted by the sound of heavy footsteps stomping down the stairwell from above.

*Who could that be?*

No one lived above him but Tareski.

'May I come in?' asked Leon nervously.

To his surprise, the old woman hesitated. 'Well, I'm not really prepared for guests right now, you see.'

The heavy footsteps, surely those of a man, came closer.

'I understand. But the builders seem to have damaged my water pipes.'

Ivana's eyebrows knotted together in surprise behind her glasses. 'But I thought they were just working on the steps?'

'Yes. Crazy, isn't it? They can't explain it either. But it's happened somehow, and now I'm without water.'

Leon didn't dare turn round. If the person who was marching down the steps couldn't see him yet, then any moment now they would reach the spot where they would be able to.

'And how can I help you?' asked Ivana.

179

'I hate to ask, but could I use your toilet?'

The look Ivana was giving him must have been the same one he had given the courier who brought the camera. Except that Leon, unlike that joker, was serious. Deadly serious. He *had* to go to Ivana's bathroom, and as quickly as possible, even if it wasn't to go to the toilet.

'Well, I . . . of course. No problem.'

Ivana moved aside and Leon slipped past her, just as the steps behind him got not only louder, but significantly quicker.

He shut the door hastily. Ideally he would have liked to look through the peephole, but that would only have made his neighbour more nervous.

'It's along there,' she said, showing him what he already knew. 'And please ignore the mess.'

'No problem. This is really very kind of you.'

Leon walked past the room that had previously contained a box and was now completely empty. The carpet billowed under his feet, and with his loose boot he had to take care not to trip.

'She's back now, by the way,' he heard Ivana say as he was about to open the bathroom door.

He whipped round to face her. 'Who?'

The old woman smiled so broadly that he saw the dentures in her upper jaw gleam.

'So you didn't see her?' she asked with a relieved smile.

Leon turned back to the living room, towards which his neighbour was pointing with her outstretched hand, and suddenly felt like his ribcage was about to break from the sheer force of his pounding heart.

*That's impossible.*

And yet there she sat. As if nothing had happened to her. As if she had never disappeared.

Full of beans.

'Come here, Alba,' called Ivana, patting her thighs as she did so. But the black cat just swished her tail, not even considering giving up her comfortable position on the armchair in front of the fire again.

# 33

Exhausted, Leon climbed down as quickly as he could. This time, though, he felt less like the shaft led down into some hidden world between worlds, and much more that it led into his subconscious.

He had locked Ivana's bathroom door, pushed the bath mat to one side and discovered a dull tile beneath, the rear edge of which jutted up a little from the floor. All he had to do was press down on it firmly and the tile came loose from its position, transforming into a lever with which to open the hatch.

With every step he took down into the darkness, the voices in his head became louder, all asking more or less the same question.

*Are you still in your right mind? Or is all this just an illusion?*

The darker it became, the more unsure Leon was as to whether he was really experiencing all this: *the dead cat, the choking chemist, the secret entrance in the bathroom.*

The cold rungs in his hand.

Once he got to the bottom, Leon put the camera headband back into position and activated the lamp, which once again would be his only light source.

He hadn't bothered closing the hatch door behind him.

It would only be a matter of time before old Helsing started to worry and went to check why he hadn't come out of the bathroom.

Leon could only hope that a decent amount of time would pass before she found a way to open the bathroom door from the outside.

He just needed a few minutes to confirm his suspicion.

*To open the door with the* DANGER *sign.*

*To find out what I did in my sleep.*

At the end of the passage, he touched the secret door's exposed input screen lightly. He had already tried so many wrong combinations that he was worried the electronic lock would block further attempts.

Leon pulled out the sheet music that he had put in his pocket in Tareski's apartment and smoothed it out.

He felt like he was holding the solution to the puzzle in his hand.

The violin is the key!

*The violin key.*

His sleepwalking self had heard Tareski's piano playing and created a memory trigger. To open the door, he didn't need to enter a password, but a series of notes.

*The ones behind the violin key!*

He looked at Tareski's sheet music, and for the first time in his life felt grateful that his adoptive parents had tortured him with trumpet lessons for years when he was a child. Without that the dots and lines would have meant nothing to him.

Voices disturbed Leon's concentration, a murmur at a distance, as soft as the sound of a television in the neighbouring apartment. But they were *voices*, plural, and one of them sounded like Ivana, as though she had fetched help and discovered the hatch in her bathroom.

*So quickly?*

Leon turned back to the secret door and the sheet music. All of a sudden his biological parents came into his mind. The accident. He wondered why these terrible memories were haunting him now, of all times. Leon stared at the sheet music in his hands, and it felt like a cog in his mind clicked into position, exposing a previously blocked chain of thoughts: *Moll.*

The surname of his first foster parents.

*The ones who sent me away. Because, in my sleep, I stood in front of their son's bed with a knife.*

*Adrian Moll.*

*A-Moll.*

*A-H-C-D-E-F-G-A*

The voice in Leon's head urging him to be quick quietened down as he pressed the corresponding buttons. When he got to the final 'A', with the noises behind him getting louder and closer, the voices in his head died away completely.

There was a sound as though someone had trodden on a cockroach, and the lock opened.

Leon put his whole body weight against the door, and a gap appeared in the wall as it opened.

It wasn't even half open before he heard the tortured whimper of a woman, and he knew that he had found her.

# 34

Opaque plastic sheeting, as if from a cold store, obstructed Leon's view of something that, fundamentally, he didn't want to see. He pictured his wife, bound and gagged, in a bare room with concrete walls and blood stains, doubled over in pain on a rusty chair.

He was right about the bound and gagged part. But the rest was even worse than he had imagined.

Leon shoved the sheeting to the side, smelled the sweat and odours of a suffering, sick person, stumbled a step forwards across the wooden floor into a room, and for a moment couldn't understand what he was seeing, for he was in . . .

*. . . my own bedroom?*

Slowly, as though in a trance, he touched the wardrobe to his left, next to a wall. Then he registered the bureau beside it, the metal chair, a few of his clothes strewn over it.

Leon's eyes darted around, searching for an anchor to keep them from the lifeless human being on the mattress. She was half-sitting, half-lying, and illuminated by a lamp on the bedside table next to the big double bed that looked exactly the same as his own. Just like almost everything down here looked like his bedroom. Someone had created the room and it was so perfect at first glance, in the otherwise bare cellar, that for the first few moments Leon had really thought he was in his own apartment.

Now, as soon as he realised it was a copy, he stumbled forwards.

'Natalie!'

It was more a croak than a scream. The shock slowed his breathing, and his movements. Leon felt like the air had transformed into syrup, as though he was only able to fight his way through it like a swimmer.

Over to the bed. To Natalie. To the blood.

She was bound in the same posture as on the photo the detective had shown him. Her arms above her head, chained to the bed-posts, her head bound with a dog collar.

'Darling, sweetheart, Natalie?'

He tried words, caresses, strokes, kisses, but he couldn't get through to her. Natalie was whimpering, but she wasn't conscious. Her head hung slackly, her chin propped against her naked chest. He touched her cheek gently, lifted her head, and a red thread of mucous freed itself from the corner of her mouth, dropping on to her chest. Her breasts were smeared with dirt and blood. The welts on her skin looked as though they had been inflicted by a riding whip.

Leon covered his face with his hands in shock.

*This wasn't me. It couldn't be. Or could it?*

'Natalie, darling. Did *I* do this?'

He lifted her chin carefully. Her right eye was buried beneath a bruise. With the other, she blinked sluggishly.

'Natalie, darling. Can you hear me?'

Even if his wife had been conscious, she wouldn't have been able to answer him. A black rubber gagging ball was in her mouth. She had bitten into it so hard that Leon feared he wouldn't be able to take it out without breaking even more of her teeth. In the end he managed it.

186

Next he inspected her ties, but to get the handcuffs off, he would need a key or a bolt cutter.

Leon looked around and reached for the bedside lamp to light under the bed. Then he stopped; there were two defunct spotlights next to a camera tripod.

*They don't belong to me. Or do they?*

He spotted a low table, covered with black latex film and with a variety of objects on top.

'Hmhmm.'

He looked at Natalie, unsure as to whether she had just groaned his name, and stroked her dull hair.

'Can you hear me?'

No reaction.

Leon promised her that he would be back soon, and went over to the table. He was repulsed by the wild collection of sex toys spread out on it: dildos, whips, lube, chains, various clamps, even a gas mask lay at the ready, along with another pair of handcuffs and keys. He picked them up and returned to Natalie.

*I didn't do this. These don't belong to me.*

He knelt down next to her and tried first her left wrist and then the other, but the key wouldn't fit, and he was unable to find any others, not even in the drawers of the nightstand, which he tore open one after the other, finding nothing but porno magazines.

'Lon?' he heard Natalie murmur next to him.

Now her groans sounded very much like his name, but beyond that he still couldn't get through to her. Leon suspected she was talking in her sleep and reacting subconsciously to his voice and touch – leaving her alone now would mean sacrificing the fragile connection.

But he didn't have a choice. He had to get help.

As quickly as he could, he hurried through the sheeting back to the secret door, only to encounter the next shock.

187

The door must have been equipped with a fire protection mechanism or something which had pushed it closed automatically and locked it. As on the outside, the inner side of the door had an entry field, but this time the electronic lock didn't react to the a-Moll combination.

Leon tried every other combination of letters he could think of. His name, Natalie's, other musical keys . . . He even typed 'help' in different languages, but all it brought him was an increasing feeling of exhaustion. He yawned, fighting the urge to lie on the floor there and then.

*Just briefly. To build up some strength.*

If Natalie hadn't called his name again, her voice filled with fear and pain and unmistakably clear this time, he might have given in to the pull threatening to make him sleep.

When he got back to his wife, she opened her uninjured eye.

Her breathing quickened erratically as she recognised him. Her ribcage rose and fell as though she was trying to draw in air before diving underwater.

'Stay calm, darling. I won't hurt you.'

*Not any more.*

She began to tug at her handcuffs.

'What is it?' he asked, then understood her panicked reaction as he saw the reflection of light in her pupils.

'Don't worry, I'm awake.' He pulled the headband with the camera down over his chin, until it hung slackly around his neck like a necklace.

'I'm not here to film you.'

*Or to hurt you.*

She didn't seem to believe him, continuing to pull at her handcuffs.

'I'm sorry, I can't open them,' Leon said resignedly. He omitted to mention that he had the same problem with the exit and that she was imprisoned here with him. Nor did he tell her that he was struggling just as much as she was to stay conscious. He would have thought that the horror he was living through right now would have activated his last survival instincts. But, instead, it seemed to have killed them off.

'Please . . . you have to . . .' groaned Natalie.

She was so weak she couldn't even finish her sentence.

'Yes. I know.'

*I have to stay awake.*

'Please don't . . .'

Leon yawned, hating himself for doing it now of all times. But as inappropriate as it was, he couldn't fight his body's need for sleep any longer without some kind of help.

'I'm so sorry,' he whispered, kissing her on the forehead. 'It will all be over soon.'

*As soon as I've found a way out of here.* He remembered Ivana and the sound of voices in the shaft, and it gave him hope.

'I'm sure they're already looking for me, Natalie.'

His wife sniffed, a bubble of snot bursting. Then she said something that tore Leon's heart in two.

'. . . hurts so much, you have to . . .'

'I will, darling. I'll stop. I'll never hurt you again.' He felt tears pricking his eyes. 'I'm so sorry. I change when I sleep. I'm no longer myself.' Leon pulled the packet of caffeine pills from his pocket. 'Here, look. These are yours, I'll take them. I'll stay awake until help comes.'

*And not sleepwalk any more. I'll never hurt you again.*

His mouth was so dry that he struggled to swallow two tablets at once, and when he had finally managed it, Natalie's eye began to twitch. It was less a question of minutes than seconds until she lost consciousness once more.

'You can't . . .' she mumbled again, but this time it sounded less like pleading. Not as though she wanted to ask him something, but instead like she wanted to tell him something.

His gaze wandered to her hand with the ripped-off thumbnail.

*What can't I do? Torture you any more?*

He didn't dare look her in the face, so great was his fear of seeing the truth.

'You have to . . .'

*Stay here? Save you? Is that what you wanted to say?*

Hope sparked inside him, and he leaned forwards to be able to understand her more clearly.

'Don't worry, sweetheart. I know I can't fall asleep again.'

'NO!'

She reared up in one final, despairing lurch, then sank down again, robbed of all energy.

'*No?* What do you mean?'

*That I should fall asleep after all? But that doesn't make any sense.*

Natalie's breathing became shallower, her voice still just a whisper, but it shattered Leon with the strength of a hurricane when she said: 'You're wrong, it's exactly the opposite.'

'The opposite? What do you mean, the opposite?' he asked anxiously, then a terrible thought sprang into the car of the rollercoaster, the tracks spiralling through Leon's mind, going up, turning in a loop and shooting into his consciousness at an unbelievable speed:

*It's not about the fact that I can't fall asleep.*

It's exactly the opposite.

*I have to stay . . . like this.*

*I CAN'T . . . WAKE UP!*

# 35

Wake up.

Just two simple words, but with the impact of an explosion.

The first explosive charges of the looming realisation detonated with painful force within Leon's head.

*I can't wake up?*

'I don't believe it,' he protested flatly, abruptly recognising how strange his voice sounded. Or had he been slurring the whole time as though he were drugged?

Leon stood up and tried to step away from the bed, but his legs refused to obey him. He was tempted to laugh, but even his lips felt numb. His face was frozen into a mask.

'Are you trying to say I'm dreaming?'

*That I'm just imagining all of this? You? The labyrinth? Our conversation?*

'No,' cried Natalie in despair.

'No what?' Leon shouted. 'What's happening to me?'

*I'm not sleeping. I'm not awake. So what am I?*

Natalie tried to answer him, but her lips moved without a sound.

'What am I?' Leon held on to her head, which was sinking downwards.

*She needs water. A doctor.*

He remembered Volwarth and how he had explained why he didn't believe Leon was capable of being violent during his sleep, and all of a sudden Leon understood what Natalie had been trying to tell him this whole time.

Of course. Volwarth.

*Not asleep. Not awake. What am I?*

The psychiatrist had given him the answer to this question just a few days ago.

*. . . strictly speaking the so-called sleepwalker isn't actually asleep. He is in another, barely researched state of consciousness between being asleep and being awake. I call it the third stage.*

A stage in which Leon, as he suddenly understood, was imprisoned. Right now. The psychiatrist had diagnosed it perfectly: *No matter what you say, I don't believe you harmed your wife in your sleep.*

Not in my sleep.

*No.*

In a conscious, criminally liable state.

Leon grabbed his head with both hands and stared at Natalie, who had plunged once more into another, hopefully pain-free world. He tried to fight the terrible truth: that he wasn't violent when he was sleepwalking.

But when he was awake!

That was when he had planned the architecture of his torture chamber, built doors in the walls and created another world beyond his apartment.

*The door behind the wardrobe, the two-way mirror, the blood in the bath . . .*

Everything he could remember right now, he had experienced not in a conscious, awake state, but as a sleepwalker.

'That can't be true,' he heard himself say as though from a great distance, but deep inside he knew it was very probably true. Volwarth had told him about similar cases.

*In the decades that I've been researching and treating parasomnias, I've encountered almost everything: people who clean their apartments in the deep-sleep phase . . .*

Or who crawl along tunnels, climb down into shafts, up ladders.

*Sleepwalkers who have coherent conversations with their partners and even answer questions.*

For example on the telephone with Natalie's best friend Anouka, Sven, the police, or over tea with Ivana.

*I had patients who did washing in the night and even operated complicated devices.*

Complicated devices like a head-mounted camera. Like a laptop in front of which Leon had sat and watched videos, in the mistaken assumption that he was awake. But he hadn't been sleeping either. Everything had really happened, except on a new, third level of consciousness, in the third stage, between being awake and asleep.

*I freed Tareski, and opened the secret door. And right now I'm standing in front of my tortured wife. Stroking her hair from her forehead, kissing her dry lips and talking to her. It's while sleepwalking that I reflect on the state I'm in. And it's a state that I can't be permitted to leave. Not yet. Because I become a danger not when I sleepwalk, but when I'm awake.*

Leon stared at Natalie, who seemed to be losing consciousness completely, while he was clearly in the process of waking up.

The whole time he had thought he could remember his dreams, but it was exactly the opposite. As a sleepwalker, he had no memory of what he had done in his conscious state.

That's why he couldn't remember the door codes or the postcard on the fridge or the fact that Sven had collected the architectural model. And that's why the policeman had asked him why he wasn't looking him in the eye. That was why Sven had fled, scared. Those two, at least, had noticed his state.

*Oh God. No.*

Leon saw the open packet of pills he had put on the nightstand.

*The more caffeine I took, the more pills I swallowed . . . the sooner I will wake up.*

*And what will happen then?*

Leon began to shiver.

*It's all exactly the opposite.*

This whole time he had been asking himself whether he was leading a double life in his sleep. Now he didn't know who he was in real life. What would he do once he regained consciousness?

Was he a perpetrator? Or a victim?

Did his presence put Natalie in danger? Or make her safe?

He could feel it wouldn't be much longer now, that he would soon leave the third stage, presumably by falling into a brief intermittent sleep before finally waking up.

*As a murderer? Or a rescuer?*

Leon knew he couldn't leave these answers to fate. He had to take precautions against the worst of all possibilities, and use the last remaining seconds he had.

He grabbed the handcuffs from the table and clapped one around his left wrist. Then, with the last of his strength, he dragged himself over to a heating pipe on the wall, approximately five paces from the bed. As he knelt down, he could no longer see Natalie, only hear her vegetative groans.

'Everything's going to be OK,' he called to her as he yawned, longer and deeper than ever before. Then, with the open end of the handcuffs, he chained himself to the pipe.

'I won't hurt you any more.'

He patted at his breast pocket, relieved to feel the fountain pen he had found in the hiding place in the adjoining passageway. Leon wrote a single word on the palm of his right hand, and four numbers on the left.

Finally, he pulled the headband with the camera back onto his head, opened his mouth, placed the handcuff key on his tongue and swallowed it.

Just a few moments later he changed states of consciousness.

# 36

Leon was awoken by a persistent ringing. For a while the shrill tones had formed part of his dream, the rest of which he could no longer remember just a few seconds after waking up. Natalie had been in it, as had a cellar, vault doors and long, dark passageways, but then the acoustic stimuli had become too intense to be filtered out by his brain. Unable to ignore the ringing of the telephone, Leon had opened his eyes.

*How is that possible?*

It was pitch black in the room, and he fumbled blindly for the light switch on the nightstand. The smell of clean washing and softener assailed his nose as he turned to the side. For an instant he felt irritated that Natalie had ignored his superstition and changed the bed-sheets during the Twelve Nights. Then he remembered that this was the least of his worries right now.

If the ringing phone in the hallway had been the cause of him waking, the sight of the empty half of the bed brought him crashing back to reality.

*I'm alone.*

'Yes, I'm coming,' he called in irritation as he flung back the blanket, wondering whether he had drunk too much or too little yesterday. His voice was hoarse, his mouth was dry, and his throat felt like he had been gargling with glass shards.

*Speaking of glass, I really need to repair that ceiling lamp.*

He looked around for his clothes. Instead of his jeans and sweatshirt, a pair of blue overalls were draped over the bureau, and the boots that he only ever wore on building sites were under the chair.

*What the hell are they doing there?*

Still drunk from a sleep that seemed to have depleted rather than increased his energy, he shuffled into the hallway naked and grabbed the telephone from the docking station.

'Yes?'

At first all he heard was a static crackle, making him think his adoptive parents, whom he had sent on a cruise as a Christmas present, were trying to call him from the ship. Then a familiar voice said hesitantly: 'It's me.'

'Sven?'

Leon pushed his hand through his unkempt hair and wondered why it felt so dirty. Stiff with dirt.

'What are you calling me in the middle of the night for?'

'The night? It's afternoon.'

'What?'

Leon went to the kitchen to get some water.

'Don't be ridiculous.'

He opened the door, causing Natalie's Van Gogh postcard with the sunflower motif to come loose from the magnetic board and fall to the floor.

'I'm not in the mood for jokes,' said Sven, as Leon stood rooted to the spot in front of the fridge.

'That's not possible.'

The green digits of the LED clock on the fridge door blurred in front of his tired eyes, but there could be no doubt that they confirmed Sven's claim: 17.22.

*That can't be possible. I can't possibly have slept that*

197

*long.* He ached so much that he felt more like he had just helped someone to move house.

'I'm really sorry,' groaned Leon. 'Did I miss an appointment or something?' He had a vague memory about a client's birthday party.

'Yes, but that's not why I'm calling.'

Even though Sven was speaking slowly, he was struggling with every other word.

'You sound agitated,' said Leon tentatively so as not to insult his friend, who couldn't stand it when people brought up the subject of his speech impediment. 'Has something happened?'

*Did we lose the commission?*

In the days since Natalie had left him for what seemed like no apparent reason, he had thrown himself into his work. He had sat working on the model day and night and hadn't left the apartment once, not even to go to the office, which was why Sven had come by to pick it up.

'It should be me asking you that. Are you feeling better now?'

'Better?' Leon opened the fridge and reached for the long-life milk. 'Why do you ask?'

'You were completely out of it last time I saw you. I felt guilty about having left you alone afterwards, but the thing with the cat was just too much.'

'When did you see me? What cat? What the hell are you talking about?' He took a slug of milk straight from the carton; while Natalie was taking her ominous 'time out', at least she couldn't have a go at him about this. It was the only advantage of his forced single existence, which he would gladly relinquish if she would just come back.

'I'm talking about yesterday,' stuttered Sven, even more agitated. 'When I brought the model back.'

'Back?'

Leon could only remember Sven having picked it up. Since then he hadn't heard anything from him.

'Yes. Back to your study,' insisted Sven. 'I put it on your desk.'

'If that's supposed to be a joke, it's not funny.'

Leon put the milk back, and as he did so he saw that the palm of his right hand was smeared with ink.

*Laptop?*

He gaped at his hand as though it didn't belong to him.

*When did I scribble the word 'laptop' on myself? And why?*

His confusion mounted when he noticed he had also used his left hand as a notepad.

*07.05.*

He couldn't imagine why he had noted down these numbers, for God knows he didn't need a reminder of this date. It was the day his biological parents had died in the car accident.

'Go and look if you don't believe me,' demanded Sven.

'For what?' asked Leon, still not really present.

'For the model.'

A sense of foreboding rose up in him as he left the kitchen, becoming terrible certainty as he entered his study.

*It's started again.*

The proof stood before him. In the middle of the desk. The model he had been working on for the last few days was back, covered by Post-its with Sven's suggested adjustments on them.

'Is everything OK?' he heard his partner ask, and answered in the affirmative even though absolutely nothing was OK any more.

'And you dropped it off with me yesterday?' he asked flatly.

'Yes.'

Leon went over to the desk and touched the roof of the accident and emergency department with his index finger.

'I was here? You spoke to me?'

'More or less. You were very incoherent and your mind seemed to be somewhere else.'

Sven's stutter was getting more pronounced. It took twice as long as it normally would for him to get the words out, but that was fine by Leon right now. His brain was working slowly, as though the handbrake was on, and the slower Sven spoke the more time he had to understand what was going on.

Leon closed his eyes. 'I'm really sorry, I don't think I even know my own name right now.'

'Well, yesterday you certainly didn't. You were a completely different person, Leon.'

*I know. I always am when I sleepwalk.*

'Don't take this the wrong way, but as your best friend I have to ask.'

'What?'

'Are you on drugs?'

Leon shook his head. 'No, that's not it.'

*It's much worse.*

Not seeming to believe him, Sven persevered. 'My brother used to take LSD. Whenever he was high, he would get this absent, empty look on his face, and talked in just the same paranoid way as you did yesterday.'

'That may well be, but I swear I'm not taking anything.'

*My dark side is something else.*

'Then it's really just because Natalie disappeared?'

'Hang on a minute, who said she disappeared?'

'You,' retorted Sven, speaking in a surprisingly loud voice now.

Leon snorted. 'That's ridiculous. She just needed a bit of time to herself. I told you about her card, remember.'

*. . . I need some space . . . to figure out where we should go from here . . .*

'That's why I'm calling, Leon. Because I don't know what to believe any more. First you tell me Natalie left you after a fight. That you woke up in the morning and she wasn't there.'

'Exactly. You told me to give her some time and distract myself with work.'

'And I thought that was what you were doing. Then you call me at the party and tell me about the injuries you supposedly inflicted on her. And yesterday you completely lose it and tell me you imprisoned her in a labyrinth behind your wardrobe.'

'Whaaat?' Leon laughed in disbelief. 'Now I should be asking *you* if you're on drugs.'

He walked from the study to get something to put on. The apartment had become cold and he was shivering.

'It's not funny, Leon, and to be honest I don't know what worries me more. The way you acted yesterday or the fact that you claim not to be able to remember it.'

'I'm not *claiming*—' Leon corrected Sven on his way into the bedroom, but he didn't manage to finish, for he felt a searing pain in the sole of his foot.

'What's wrong?' Sven asked as he heard Leon cursing.

'Sorry, I trod on something.'

Leon bent down, unable to believe what he had in his hands.

The last time he had worn such a device was many years ago, during the therapy sessions with Dr Volwarth.

'So, anyway, you were completely out of it,' Sven continued, his words accompanied by a gradually surging tinnitus in Leon's ears; a sure sign he had a migraine coming on.

*Or worse.*

With the headband that he had just found on the floor,

201

he was holding further proof in his hands that his nocturnal phases had started again.

*When did I buy this camera?*

The lens of the motion-activated head camera was smudged and a cable hung loose at the side, as though it had been put together in a hurry. By someone who hadn't been concentrating that much, because he was under massive stress.

*Or because he wasn't conscious.*

'You even wanted to show me a video you supposedly filmed of you looking for Natalie in your sleep.'

*A video?*

Along with the tinnitus, a surreal, schizophrenic feeling was welling up in Leon. On the one hand, everything Sven was saying seemed to make sense. On the other, it was as though his friend was speaking to him in a foreign language.

He clamped the telephone between his chin and shoulder so that he had both hands free to inspect the headband. If Sven was talking about a video, there must be some kind of replay function.

Leon was just about to go back into the study to start his computer when he remembered the word on his right palm.

*Laptop.*

There was only one portable computer in the apartment.

'Are you still there?' he heard Sven ask.

Without answering, he went into the bedroom. He pushed the chair to the side and picked up the carefully folded but completely soiled overalls from the desk.

*What the hell . . .?*

He had expected to find Natalie's laptop beneath them. Not the USB stick attached to it, blinking rhythmically.

Leon opened the laptop and gave a start when, with a gentle hum, it awoke from standby mode.

'Hey, Leon, why have you gone quiet?'

*Because I can't find the words. No, more than that. I'm afraid I can't find part of myself.*

A replay window for video files had appeared on the screen, and all of a sudden Leon no longer felt cold. His whole body was numb, insensitive to external stimuli.

He balled his right fist, pressed his fingernails hard into his palm, and before he could even ask the question as to whether he should dare do it, he had stretched his hand out and moved the mouse towards PLAY.

'What's wrong with you?' asked Sven anxiously.

*Nothing. Nothing's wrong.*

The video file didn't start. Instead, an entry field appeared, demanding a password.

*Damn it, how am I supposed to be able to remember a password I chose in my sleep?*

Leon held his breath in shock. Slowly, he turned the palm of his left hand up and stared at the two pairs of digits, separated by a full stop.

*07.05*

'I'll call you back in a minute,' he said to Sven, hanging up. Then he typed the date of the car accident into the laptop.

The replay started at once.

# 37

At first there was nothing to see but dark flecks, twitching across the screen in various degrees of shadow. Then, as the sound of rattling breaths suddenly strained the loudspeakers, the image became brighter. Threads of light snaked across the picture like the tentacles of a jellyfish.

The contrasts sharpened and the contours of a room became increasingly clear, reminding Leon of his bedroom. The large bed, filmed from the perspective of someone sitting on the floor, certainly looked identical to the one he had woken up in a little earlier.

There was a jolt on the screen, and while the camera focused on a table leg, Leon heard a metallic clanking that sounded like a chain – reminding him of something that he couldn't figure out at first.

*Handcuffs?*

Then he heard a voice that wasn't his own and which seemed to be coming from the bed. The person lying on it wasn't visible, but Leon didn't need to see to know who was sobbing his name.

*Natalie!*

He stared at the monitor with his eyes wide, and suddenly a flood of memories almost knocked him off the chair. It wasn't a dream!

*I was there. In the labyrinth. Behind the door. With her.*

He vaguely remembered a door behind the wardrobe, the dark passageways and the secret code (a-Moll), and the handcuffs he had used to chain himself to a heating pipe.

*To prevent the worst from happening.*

Leon felt as though someone had managed to install a dream camera in his head, saving the images he normally forgot right after waking up.

*But I wasn't sleeping. And I wasn't awake either.*

On the recording, the rasping breaths turned into a choking sound. He instinctively put his hands to his throat, suspecting he knew why it was so raw and why it still hurt to swallow.

*The key. Natalie's life insurance policy.*

He stared fixedly at the monitor.

The picture began to shake, and he heard a guttural groan. Then the camera tipped down and Leon saw a wave of vomit flow over the workers' boots on his feet.

As he continued to retch on the video, Leon groped his hand over to the overalls next to him on the desk and felt the dried sick on the trouser legs. A quick glance at the boot under the chair confirmed that they were soiled too. And one of them was missing the bootlace.

'No, no!' roared Leon at the laptop, as though he could somehow prevent himself from picking the key out of the pool of vomit.

*Please, don't let me do it. Let it stop*, he pleaded in his thoughts. But it didn't stop. The recording ran on mercilessly. The image was blurred because the camera was so close to the pipe, but the audio was clearer than ever now.

A handcuff scraped across metal, then clicked loudly, and when the camera abruptly rushed upwards Leon knew he had freed himself from his shackles.

*My God.*

The sight that revealed itself to him from a standing

perspective was exactly as Leon had expected: Natalie lay stretched out on the bed as though on a crucifix, chained with a dog collar. But unlike in his dream, she was fully conscious.

The camera moved closer to her face, so close that Leon could make out the fine pores on her nose and the encrusted blood on her chin covering the small freckle he had kissed so often in these last years. She blinked, blinded by the light of the head camera. Fat tears tumbled down from both the open and the injured eye.

'Leon?' she asked, and the camera image moved up and down affirmatively.

'Leon, I'm so sorry.'

*You? You're sorry?*

She sounded exhausted and breathless, but not panicked. Like a human being who had come to the end of their journey.

'I didn't mean to betray you?'

'Betray me?' Leon asked the monitor. With tears in his eyes, he touched the crackling surface of the laptop and traced his index finger along his wife's split lip.

'Leon, please. Forgive me.'

'Oh God, darling.'

*Of course. Whatever you've done, I'll forgive you,* he thought. *All I want is to have you back here with me.*

But his alter ego, down in the labyrinth, didn't seem to want to forgive his victim. A shadow fell across his wife's beaten face.

'Please, please don't . . .'

'No, no more pain . . .'

They both began to speak at the same time.

Natalie was pleading at the camera and Leon at his computer. He prayed that he was in one of his sleep paralyses right now, one from which he could only free himself with loud screams. But unlike usual, he had long realised that this wasn't a dream.

Something golden flashed on the monitor. It was a few moments before Leon recognised the tip of his own fountain pen.

*Please . . . No!*

'I love you,' they said, almost simultaneously. He, up in his bedroom. She, down in the torture chamber. And while Leon screamed out his despair, Natalie only sounded sad and resigned. He could see in her face that she knew what was awaiting her.

Natalie closed her uninjured eye just before it happened. Just before he rammed the fountain pen into her neck, with such force that almost half its length disappeared.

'*Noooooo!*'

Leon screamed, jumped up, grabbed the metal chair he had been sitting on and threw it across the room against the wall mirror. Cracks spread across the glass like a spider's web, then jagged-edged splinters came away, falling to the floor. At the same time, four hundred litres of water gushed onto the bedroom floor. The metal chair had rebounded from the wall into Natalie's aquarium, smashing a section of the glass panes.

*Please no. Don't let it be true.*

In tears, Leon buried his face in his hands, biting his fingers so hard that the pain would have ripped him out of the dream if it had been one. But it was real. The fountain pen in Natalie's neck, her punctured windpipe, her choked wheezing, the whistle with every breath that became first longer, then quieter, her slowly twitching body, her head slumping forwards. And the unbearable silence that set in, still far from being the end of the recording.

Leon continued to look through his fingers, covering his eyes, unable to bear the sight for longer than a second at a time. The monitor picture with Natalie's motionless body in the centre shook and blurred, but this time it wasn't down to the recording. Leon's eyes had transformed into torrents, and his body was shaking convulsively.

He wiped his tears away with the back of his hand, and as he did so his gaze fell on the business card next to the computer.

*Kroeger?*

Leon had never seen the card before, never heard the name, and didn't know what it was doing there, but the embossed signet on the front told him what he had to do next.

*The police! I have to call the police!*

To use the telephone, he needed both hands. He was in shock, and so overwhelmed that he had even forgotten the number of the emergency services. By the time he remembered, there was a dramatic change on the screen.

His alter ego in the torture dungeon seemed to have finally had his fill of the sight of Natalie's motionless body, and moved just as the camera started to go into standby mode. The image flickered back on.

*What now? What am I going to do now?*

The camera panned left behind the bed to the spotlight and table, which Leon had a vague memory of. The sex toys spread out on it also seemed eerily familiar.

'I'm sorry,' he sobbed.

*What have I done? And why?*

He didn't understand why she had asked for his forgiveness. And he was unable to believe what happened next.

Just as at the entrance, there was plastic sheeting hanging from the ceiling at the far side of the room. It parted in front of the camera as though moved by some invisible hand, exposing a door. Just one kick with his boot and it sprang open.

*There's a second exit? I could have just gone to fetch help?*

Leon's despair had reached a new level that usually only suicidal people reach. The telephone in his hand had been forgotten for now.

*Where am I going?*

Behind the door some steps, steep like a fire ladder, headed upwards in a zigzag pattern. Leon heard himself panting after just the first few steps.

He didn't want to watch any more. He wanted this to be the end. Over. Finished. Like the rest of his life.

But his sleepwalking self was nowhere near finished. Step by step, he climbed up. Step by step, his breathing on the tape became more laboured, and even in the bedroom an invisible clamp tightened around Leon's ribcage.

*What else have I done?*

Once he got to the top of the steps, the picture became blurry again, just as at the beginning of the recording. Leon leaned towards the flickering monitor, so close that the picture before him resolved into individual dots.

The spotlight of the head camera focused on something that looked like a chipboard panel. Leon saw himself stretch his hand out and press the panel inwards.

On the video, another secret door opened.

At the same time Leon felt a gust of cold air at the back of his neck, and a shadow wandered across the screen. Then he suddenly heard everything in duplicate.

The creak of the secret door opening.

The crunch of the boots on the glass shards.

And even though there could only be one possible explanation for this, it took Leon far too long to react.

He stared at the screen, paralysed by the sight of a young man's back, a man who was staring at a laptop monitor, not wanting to believe that he wasn't watching a stranger.

But himself.

He didn't want to believe that he wasn't watching a recording. But the present.

Late, much too late, he turned to the hole in the wall from which until just a moment ago his splintered bedroom mirror had been hanging, where a man was now standing in a puddle on the flooded parquet floor. He was around the same height as Leon, of a similar stature. With brown hair, blue overalls, a sweatshirt and a pair of worker's boots, the right one of which was missing its bootlace.

The stranger had on a headband with a camera attached to it, the lamp of which was shining right into Leon's eyes. As a result, he was unable to see the man's face as he ran forward, as quick as lightning, to tear Leon into a maelstrom of pain. And a whole new dimension of darkness.

# 38

Like sleep, the process of waking up is an under-researched medical mystery. So as not to be woken by each and every noise, the brain restricts the intensity of external stimuli. However, it isn't in a permanently muffled state. Several times per hour, it shifts for a few moments into a near-conscious mode. In this brief phase the brain stretches its feelers into the world outside the dream, like a submarine does its periscope, to check if it would be advisable to change the state of consciousness, for example if the sleeping person is in danger.

Generally speaking, outside the near-conscious sleep stage only very strong stimuli are able to wake the person from sleep. The loud ringing of an alarm clock, for example, or a stream of cold water or intense pain – like the pain that brought Leon Nader back to reality.

For a while he had tried to fight against the thing around his neck, which was now pulling him upwards. Even with his eyes shut, he had realised that the pain shooting along his spine would only become more bearable if he gave into the pull at his head. Besides this, the more he struggled, the harder it was to breathe.

Hearing his neck vertebrae crunch, Leon opened his eyes wide. He was sat on the floor completely naked, his legs stretched out, his back against the bed, but if he didn't want his own weight to break his neck, he would have to get up as quickly as possible.

His legs were like rubber. At first he only managed to get to his knees. The pressure around his throat lessened, but the fought-for space quickly disappeared.

Leon looked to the hook on the ceiling, where the previous tenant's chandelier had hung and over which the rope of his noose was being pulled.

The stranger who had come into his bedroom through the secret passageway behind the mirror stood in front of the bureau with an expressionless gaze, pulling at the other end of the noose like a hoist.

Leon doubted that he had the strength to stand, but he had no choice. If he didn't want to suffocate, he had to straighten up.

'Stop,' he croaked, as Natalie's murderer forced him to his feet.

*Oh God. What now?*

To try to keep his balance, he flailed his arms, which strangely weren't tied. His hands, however, were encased in thick latex gloves. Whenever he tried to grab the rope over his head, the psychopath at the other end pulled even more strongly, making Leon fear that his larynx would burst.

'No,' coughed Leon, choking. 'Please don't.'

He rolled his eyes in panic and noticed a chair next to him. He had thrown it against the mirror earlier, but now it was upright, and within his grasp.

As if wanting to reward him for the discovery, the killer loosened the rope, and Leon hooked the chair towards him with his leg. But as soon as he had, the man mercilessly pulled him upwards once more. And he only stopped once Leon had clambered on to the chair.

'Please, carry on,' the man laughed, fastening the rope to

the radiator beneath the window with a complicated-looking knot.

Not just his voice, but his appearance in general seemed familiar to Leon – aside from the fact, of course, that the man had made a great deal of effort to copy Leon's physical appearance.

'Who are you?' Leon croaked, craning his neck a little. He was surprised he could even get a word out. To stop him from freeing the rope from the hook by jumping, the maniac had pulled it so tight that he had to stand on tiptoes if he wanted to avoid losing consciousness.

The man trying to hang him was his age, perhaps a little younger, and apart from a slightly over-large nose and missing left earlobe, there was nothing remarkable about his appearance.

'I have a delivery for you,' he laughed, waving a CD case that he had just pulled from the breast pocket of his overalls.

Then he left the room briefly, returning with a kitchen stool in his hand. His soles squeaked on the wet floor.

He sat down in front of the laptop and put the disc in.

*Please, God, make it stop. Don't let it get any worse.*

From where he was, Leon could see the right half of the monitor. Every time he moved his head he ran the risk of lacerating his neck, but he still wrenched it to the side when Natalie's face appeared on the screen. Her right eye was shimmering violet, her eyelids were swollen shut, and when she tried to speak her tongue jutted against a cracked front tooth.

Leon couldn't bear to see the pictures that reminded him of his darkest nightmares, and of the fact that he would never see his wife alive again.

But even without the images, the mental torture didn't stop, for there was nothing Leon could do to stop himself from hearing. The psychopath had turned the volume of the video up to the maximum so that Leon didn't miss a single word of Natalie's acoustic goodbye note, which she had dictated for him in a trembling voice:

*Leon, I'm so sorry*, she began. *I'm a coward, I know. I should be telling you all this to your face. That's what you deserved. But I don't have the strength, so I'm choosing this unusual way. So that, even if it's impersonal, you at least hear it in my own words.*

'Stop the tape!' gasped Leon in the break between her words.

*But I'm not sure if I'm going to have enough strength to put this confession in our letterbox. If it turns out I'm too cowardly even for that, then I'll at least leave you a card on the kitchen door.*

Leon closed his eyes, then had to open them again at once, feeling like he was about to lose his balance and strangle himself.

*Right now, while I'm recording this, you're still sleeping,* he heard Natalie say.

*I'm going to pack my things in a moment, and hope you won't wake up while I'm doing it. I think you're having nightmares again. Your night terrors have got worse, presumably because you can sense something's wrong. How right you are, my darling. And it's my fault and mine alone.*

Leon turned back towards the bureau, in front of which the killer was standing. He had stopped the recording. The frozen image of Natalie suggested that she had recorded it with her mobile in her dark room. Leon could make out the photographic equipment in the background.

'This is very embarrassing,' grinned Natalie's killer all of a sudden. 'But could I use your toilet? It's just that I have diarrhoea.'

As he chuckled, Leon finally recognised who was doing

all of this to him. 'I'll leave the entertainment running for you,' said the man who had once pretended to be a courier. Once he had started the video again, he went to the bedroom door.

Feeling faint, Leon had to watch the psychopath leave the room knowing full well that it didn't give him any advantage. He tried to pull himself up on the rope, but he was exhausted from over-exertion and lack of sleep. His arms were too heavy; he would never be able to do it. There was no point contemplating the backrest of the chair; it would tip over as soon as he stepped on it. And he couldn't jump either.

*There are no words to apologise for what I've done to you*, Natalie continued. *So I'll just come out and say it: I betrayed you. With a man I've fallen for. No, a man I* fell *for, past tense. The two of us never had to speak about my desires, Leon. We both know I have a dark side that's unknown to you. One I lived out secretly. At first it was wild, exciting and exotic. At first I thought he was fulfilling my needs. But I was wrong. And now everything, as you can see, has got completely out of control.*

She pointed to her injuries and her face contorted into a pain-filled smile.

*His name is Siegfried von Boyten. He's the owner of this building, and he's the starting point, the core and the source of all my lies. We never applied for this apartment, my darling. He provided it for me; I had already been with him for a while by then.*

Her confession was like a knife to the gut. Leon wondered how much more he could take.

*Siegfried approached me in Dr Volwarth's waiting room. He was receiving psychiatric treatment. Just like me.*

Natalie swallowed heavily.

*Yes, I'm in therapy, and I'm afraid that's far from the*

*only thing I've kept from you. My desires became more and more extreme, more and more bizarre. I was scared of talking to you about it. I was afraid of myself. I was with another doctor originally, but he referred me to Dr Volwarth. Back then we weren't yet married, so he didn't realise I knew you. He helped me a great deal, by the way.*

She paused, then added quietly: *The man who made me pregnant.*

'No!' screamed Leon, as loudly as the noose around his neck would allow.

He felt an icy gust of air rush through his body. His legs became numb, he couldn't feel his toes any more, couldn't hold himself up any longer. Pressure forced down on his Adam's apple as he sank, but it was no longer the noose choking him; it was Natalie's confession.

*Do you understand now why I can't look you in the eyes? I didn't just betray you. I let you believe that we had lost our child. But it was his baby I aborted. And it looks like now I'm getting the punishment I deserve. Von Boyten is a psychopath, Leon. He beat me, tortured me and raped me.*

She held her thumb up to the camera.

*This has nothing to do with my fantasies. Boyten is a sadist who loves dominating weak people. Tormenting them and watching. He's a perverse voyeur, and assumes other identities to manipulate people. Once he pretended to be a courier to demonstrate to me how powerful he is; he wanted to be close to me while you were standing alongside.*

Leon shook his head, disbelieving, uncomprehending. With

216

every movement, the noose cut deeper into his neck, but he didn't care. Nothing had any meaning any more. Not even the fact that he wasn't a twisted murderer after all. Natalie had betrayed him and she was dead. And in a few moments he would share her fate.

*I think Siegfried has a spare key to our apartment, and he snoops around when I'm not there. I have no idea how he does it, but he's like one of those ghosts of the Twelve Nights you told me about, in the very worst form. First he poisoned my fish. Then me. And finally us.*

Leon looked at the destroyed aquarium and wondered if the water damage had reached Ivana below yet, and if she would fetch help.

*He watches me. He knows things I've never told him. About my father. And about your sleep disturbances.*

From the tone of Natalie's voice, it sounded like she was coming to the end of what she wanted to say.

*I love you, Leon. I tried so often to end things with him, and I accepted your proposal far too quickly because I thought that he would let me go if we were married. But we had already gone too far. He wouldn't take no for an answer. Until today. Now I'm not giving him a choice. I'll go to the police and report him. I've got no idea what I'll do after that, and I don't know when I'll speak to you again. I'm so ashamed, and so scared, but it's what I deserve.*

'No,' retorted Leon, pain shooting up his legs. He couldn't stay on his tiptoes for much longer.

*No one deserves this.*

Everything she said, everything she had done, none of it changed his feelings for her. Not even in the face of the death that had entered their lives because of her betrayal.

*Especially not in the face of death.*

Under normal circumstances, he would never have been able to forgive her. They would have divorced, broken off all contact, moved to different cities and only heard from each other if a trick of fate had wanted it to be so.

But, and Leon was sure of this, they would never have stopped loving each other.

*Don't wait for me*, demanded Natalie. If she had seemed surprisingly composed up until this point in the recording, now the dam broke. She looked upwards and jutted out her lower lip, but otherwise made no attempt to stop the flow of her tears.

*I'm not worth it. I know that we have no future any more. I've destroyed everything. But if my betrayal was good for anything, it was to show me how much I love you. How much I will always love you.*

'How sweet.'

Leon twisted around to the door, and in his shock at the psychopath's words started to teeter. Cold sweat broke out on his forehead. He didn't know whether the man whose name he now knew had been standing in the doorway for a while, or whether he had only just come back.

Natalie's lips formed into one last kiss. Then they contorted, and beneath the tortured grimace Leon was able to recognise an echo of the smile he had fallen in love with years before.

There was a noise, and the monitor went black. Siegfried von Boyten sat down in front of the computer again.

'Why?' rasped Leon.

No reaction. Natalie's murderer brushed his fingers over the keyboard, humming.

*Why are you doing this? Why are you destroying our lives?*

*And why did you just show me that?*

Leon watched as von Boyten took the DVD out of the laptop and opened an editing program, then realised that the maniac had not played the recording for his benefit.

*He just wanted to make a copy.*

Clearly it was the soundtrack that held the sadist's interest, as he now began to edit it. Siegfried made a few, purposeful cuts, shortening the entire audio file to the length of a few seconds. In the end, only a sound file remained, its meaning distorted, with an aim as gruesome as everything else the psychopath had done.

# 39

*Right. Left. And right again.*

*Regardless of how great the pain is. Regardless of how much blood there is.*

Leon had realised what the sadist intended to do, which was why he didn't have any choice. He had to move while there was still time. Before Siegfried von Boyten succeeded in committing the perfect murder.

*No!* he heard Natalie scream, and knew it was only in his memory. The memory of a dream in which he was in a basement room that looked exactly like this bedroom here.

*So the bastard could film the video clip there that he then forced me to watch.*

*No!* screamed Natalie even louder in his thoughts. In his dream (*no, in the third stage!*), he had thought she was afraid of him. Of him falling asleep again and doing something to her. But it was exactly the other way around. He was supposed to wake up and help her. Because as a sleepwalker, he was useless and unable to rescue her.

Von Boyten had gone back into the corridor, so Leon couldn't see what he was doing, but he didn't need to. He could *hear* it.

'Hello, you've reached Natalie and Leon. Please leave your message after the tone.'

*He's playing it on to the answerphone machine! Fuck, he's PLAYING IT ON TO MY ANSWERPHONE MACHINE!*

Leon was right. A few seconds later, he heard the compilation of Natalie's last words in that distorted tone typical of recorded messages.

*Leon, darling . . . I'm so sorry. There are no words to apologise for what I've done, so I'll just come out and say it: I betrayed you. With a man I've fallen for. He's fulfilling my needs. We have no future any more. I don't know when I'll speak to you again.*

'You won't get away with this,' croaked Leon, choking. But he knew he was wrong.

A computer expert would be able to recognise the edits on the soundtrack, but who would even bother to order such an expensive analysis with an obvious suicide? The case was clear-cut: the cheating wife admits her betrayal. Her husband loses his mind. A crime of passion. Then, to end it all, he hangs himself. It was the oldest story in the world.

*And to clear up any last doubts, there is even a video of proof. Oh God.*

Everyone who saw the recording of Natalie's execution would think it was Leon who had rammed the pen into her neck. After all, even he had fallen for the deception at first. Admittedly Siegfried would have to erase the final seconds after Natalie's murder – the part in which he climbed through the door behind the mirror and into the bedroom – but that was child's play compared to how he had directed their lives for the whole of the last year.

*Left. Right.*

*Keep moving. Just don't make a sound. Even if the pain tears you apart.*

Leon was shaking all over. He stopped, so as not to pass out from the pain, while in the hallway Siegfried checked the recording one more time.

By now he had managed to manipulate the time record on the answer machine. According to the digital voice, Natalie's call had been received several days ago.

*Long before her death.*

*Left. Right. Turn again.*

Even with the pain, Leon's thoughts wouldn't stop coming.

*Damn it, there are even witnesses to incriminate me. I admitted to Sven that I had hit Natalie and filmed myself in the labyrinth.*

But at least Sven would confirm his confused mental state.

*Left. Right. Left.*

Leon couldn't bear the torment for much longer. Neither the physical nor the mental.

*How much longer is this going to go on?* he screamed in his thoughts, biting his tongue until it bled.

*How many video recordings did you fake? How much longer are you going to manipulate me for?*

He heard steps from the hallway, saw a shadow and turned towards the bedroom door.

'Right then, now it's your turn—' said von Boyten, stopping short, his sarcastic grin dying away mid-sentence.

Leon was sure that von Boyten would have kicked the chair away from under his feet there and then if he hadn't been so shocked by the sight before him.

*Left. Right. And left again.*

'What are you doing?' screamed Siegfried, hit by the realisation that his perfect plan wasn't functioning so perfectly any more.

*Right. Left again.*

*No matter how much it hurts.*

Leon had lacerated his neck with the rope, and even now he didn't stop moving his head.

*Left. Right.*

The coarse rope was scraping against his raw flesh like

steel wool. Blood was running down over his chest and stomach, so much that he could even feel it on his scrotum, dropping down in gloopy threads on to the seat of the chair.

'Stop it. Stop that at once.'

Leon had no intention of stopping. Every cut into his flesh was a signal that he was still alive. Better than that: he was creating proof that he had struggled. No forensic in the world could overlook this. No one would assume suicide with these injuries. If there had been more time he would have taken the gloves off too, but wounds on the hands could also be seen as the suicide's attempt to escape after a change of mind. But with the lacerations to his neck, this assumption wasn't possible.

'Fuck. You arsehole.'

Leon started to laugh.

Bound, hung up and bleeding, he was at the pervert's mercy, but he still had the advantage. It was something the sadist just couldn't bear. He had wanted to humiliate, control and feed off his victim's death throes, but Leon was changing the course of events.

'Now I'm really going to hurt you,' screamed von Boyten, lifting his hands above his head in despair. 'Now you're going to know what pain is, you stupid bastard.'

His unremarkable face had transformed into an ugly mask. Spit collected in the corners of his mouth as he shouted. He wandered aimlessly around the room.

Siegfried appeared not to know what to do next, and this made him furious. That and the fact that Leon had lost all his fear of death and was laughing mockingly in von Boyten's face.

Siegfried stopped in front of the chair. His face reddened, the pulse on his neck pumped, and his eyes became dull, losing any hint of human emotion. Leon knew he had only seconds left. Von Boyten was no longer following a plan, apart from the desire to kill him in the most torturous manner possible.

Whatever the murderer wanted to do, Leon knew he couldn't let the psychopath out of his reach. Even in his rage, Siegfried had not made the mistake of getting close to Leon's arms. Von Boyten had stopped for a moment a metre from the chair, but he turned away again, towards the rope tied to the heating pipe. Leon could almost hear his thoughts: was there another position in which he could torture Leon better?

*It's now or never.*

Just one more step and it would be too late.

'Hey,' yelled Leon, but his voice wasn't strong enough to get through to the crazed killer, which turned out to be a stroke of luck. If Siegfried had turned round, he would have seen the imminent danger. But instead, when Leon clamped his legs around von Boyten's neck it took him completely by surprise.

Leon, who had nothing more to lose, had jumped from the chair with the very last of his energy and was holding the murderer in a stranglehold with his thighs.

Siegfried let out a cry of shock and stumbled backwards, then instinctively tried to rear up and shake the burden from his shoulders – which was his mistake.

If he had kept calm or fallen forwards, Leon's fate would have been sealed. But he was carrying his victim piggyback. The rope lost its tension and began to ride up the hook on the ceiling, eventually looping free.

Siegfried lost his untied boot, stumbled over it and twisted as he fell, taking Leon down with him.

Realising that he could be strangled in a matter of moments, Leon reached up to grasp the rope and was stunned when it didn't stop his fall. Holding the rope, his feet hit the chair, and he fell hard, head first, on to the wet parquet. His last thought was – *The rope came free from the hook* – before the world behind his eyes transformed into a ball of fire.

# 40

Leon couldn't see anything, couldn't catch his breath, and the pain had reached a new high point. But he was still expecting the torture to get much worse, as soon as von Boyten had struggled to his feet beside him.

For now he was satisfying himself with hefty kicks to Leon's lower body. Protecting his genitals with one hand and holding the other in front of his face, Leon wondered why Siegfried's kicks were so untargeted.

He tried to open his eyes. The world looked blurred, which was no great surprise given the impact the fall must have had on his head.

*What is he waiting for?*

Von Boyten screamed something that Leon was unable to understand, because the whistling inside his head had reached the volume of an exploding kettle. He tried to prop himself up, and his hands touched a puddle that he hoped wasn't blood.

Siegfried's kicks, meanwhile, were becoming quicker but weaker. And his cries louder.

*What is he going to do? What does he want, for me to look him in the eyes as I die?*

Leon's vision had improved marginally, so now he was at least able to make out the contours of Siegfried's body.

They were lying next to each other as if lovers, on their sides, their faces turned towards each other.

Leon blinked, but the sensation that he was seeing the killer through a pane of glass refused to disappear. Because it *couldn't*.

No more than von Boyten could stop kicking around wildly and making incomprehensible noises.

Unlike Leon, he had tried to brace his fall with his hands. Angel fish, Natalie's favourite, needed a high-sided aquarium, and Siegfried's arms hadn't been long enough to stop a tall, still-standing spike of glass at the front of it from slicing through his throat as he fell into the remains of the aquarium.

*But he's still alive. The bastard's still alive.*

Leon struggled to his knees. Thick blood was seeping from von Boyten's throat, and he was twitching uncontrollably.

'Hah!' Leon loosened the noose around his neck and sucked air into his lungs, gurgling.

Loud. Despairing. Hysterical.

With both hands he grabbed the dying Siegfried von Boyten by the hair and roared his murdered wife's name again and again. When his voice failed him, he smashed von Boyten's head back on the shards of glass, impaling him even deeper.

He waited until the twitching had stopped, until Siegfried had drawn his last breath.

Then he stood up, the shards of glass cutting his bare feet.

Bloody footprints marked his path across the hallway into the stairwell, and down the steps. It was too late. The working day had come to an end. There were no more workers to be seen.

'Help!' he screamed. Then again, alternating it with Natalie's name. He rang the bell of every apartment door, not waiting to see if anyone opened up, instead stumbling to the exit and out on to the street.

227

Snow blew into his face.

A couple gave a start at the sight of him, and passers-by gaped in astonishment as he ran naked and covered in blood through the cold, screaming for help.

In front of the supermarket on the corner, he broke down.

No one spoke to him. No one wanted to get too close to a man who was clearly mentally disturbed, but Leon could see a cluster of curious people gathering around. Many had pulled out their mobile phones.

'She's still downstairs,' Leon heard himself scream.

*Quickly. I have to tell them before I don't have any strength left.*

'Hurry. He's freezing to death,' he heard a woman shout. Cars were beeping. Youths were laughing and taking photos.

'Natalie's downstairs. In the labyrinth.'

*They have to look for her. Maybe she can still be saved.*

Leon was shaking as though he had just received an electric shock, and then felt a blanket being laid on him. Someone asked what his name was, but that wasn't important, so he just said: 'Push the wardrobe to the side and go into the labyrinth. You'll find Natalie behind the secret door.'

'Yes, we'll do that. But for now you need to come with us.'

Car doors slammed, then everything around him was flashing in blue and white, and the man who was wearing a red high-visibility vest with a white cross grasped him by the shoulders while another grabbed his feet. Leon swayed.

'Don't you understand? He rammed a pen into her neck. The code for the secret door is a-Moll. You have to hurry.'

'Of course. Calm down now,' said the man, belting him securely to the stretcher in the ambulance. 'Do you know who you are?'

Leon tried to sit up and was pulled back by the restraints. 'It was Siegfried. Siegfried von Boyten.'

228

'Is that your name?'

'No. His father built the house. He knew the secret world behind the wardrobe.'

'Of course.'

'Noooo!' screamed Leon, shaking at the restraints on his arm.

*They don't believe me. Oh God.*

'Please, don't waste any time. Natalie might still be alive. You have to look for her.'

'In the secret world behind the wardrobe. Of course.'

He felt something cold on his arm, then a prick, and the ambulance was moving, its siren blaring.

# 41

The patient hadn't even been on the ward for half an hour, and already he was causing trouble. Sister Susan had *tasted* it, almost as soon as the ambulance opened its doors and the stretcher was pushed out.

She could always taste it when problems rolled into the psychiatric department. She would get this strange sensation in her mouth, as though she was chewing on aluminium foil. It could even be unleashed by patients who at first glance seemed more like victims and not aggressive in the slightest; much like the man who had just activated the alarm in Room 1310.

*And at five to eight, of all times.*

If he could just have waited another five minutes, Susan would have been on her break. Instead, she had to rush along the corridor on an empty stomach. Not that she had much of an appetite in the evenings anyway. She took great care not to gain weight, even though she wasn't much bigger than some of the anorexia patients being treated on the ward. The tiny salad and half an egg were part of her evening routine – as was, admittedly, a paranoid schizophrenic with hallucinations, but she would have gladly relinquished the latter.

The patient had been found lying naked in the snow in

front of a supermarket, covered in blood and with lacerations on his feet. He had appeared bedraggled, disorientated and dehydrated, but his gaze was alert and steady, his voice clear, and his teeth (teeth, as far as Susan was concerned, were always a sure indication of the state of the soul) showed no signs of alcohol, nicotine or substance abuse.

*And yet I could still taste it*, she thought, with one hand on her bleeper and the other on her bunch of keys.

Susan unlocked the door and entered the room.

The scene before her was so bizarre that she stood in shock for a moment before pressing the bleeper to call the security team, who were trained especially for situations such as these.

'I can prove it,' screamed the naked man in front of the window. He was standing in a pool of vomit.

'Of course you can,' answered the sister, taking care to keep her distance.

Her words sounded rehearsed rather than genuine, because Susan had indeed rehearsed them and didn't intend them to be genuine, but in the past she had often been able to win time with empty platitudes.

Not this time, though.

Later, in its final report, the inquiry panel would establish that the cleaning woman had been listening to music on an MP3 player, something strictly forbidden during working hours. When her supervisor came by unexpectedly to do a hygiene check, she had hidden the device in the water meter cupboard next to the shower.

But in the moment of crisis it was a mystery to Sister Susan as to how the patient had come into possession of the electronic device. He had ripped open its battery compartment and was holding a bent alkaline battery, which he must have chewed open with his teeth. Although Susan couldn't actually see it, she pictured the viscous battery acid flowing down over the edges like marmalade.

'Everything's going to be OK,' she said, trying to placate him.

'No, nothing's going to be OK,' the man protested. 'Listen to me. I'm not crazy. I tried to throw up to get it out of my stomach, but maybe I've already digested it. Please. You have to take an X-ray. You have to X-ray my body. The proof is inside me!'

He screamed and screamed until, eventually, the security team came in and restrained him.

But they were too late. By the time the doctors rushed into the room, the patient had long since swallowed the battery.

'So, now you need to push me into the Tube,' he announced triumphantly as he was pressed back on to the bed.

'I tied myself up when I was sleepwalking, down in the labyrinth, do you see? And because Siegfried was just pretending to be me, the handcuff key must still be in my stomach.'

'Sister, inform radiology,' said one of the doctors, shaking his head.

'And prepare for a stomach pumping,' another added. 'We have to get the battery out before it releases too much acid.'

'Fuck the acid,' screamed Leon. 'It's about the key.'

His bed was pushed out of the room.

'You'll find the handcuff keys in my stomach or my bowels, and when you do please—' Leon grabbed the hand of the doctor who was walking to the right-hand side of his bed. He had more hair on his face than on his head and a moustache that couldn't hide his cleft lip.

'Please go to my apartment and push the wardrobe back,' Leon pleaded with him. 'If it won't move, then you

232

can climb into the labyrinth through Frau Helsing's bathroom.'

'Into the labyrinth?' asked the bearded man, introducing
himself as Dr Meller.

'That's what I call it, yes. I can draw it for you. At the
end of the first shaft there's a fork in the path that leads
to a secret door.'

*And to my wife's corpse.*

Leon closed his eyes in exhaustion as he began to realise
that he wouldn't even believe himself. But it was too late
anyway. If Natalie hadn't died immediately after the stab-
bing, there was no chance she was still alive after all this
time.

'Do you mean the door with the DANGER sign?' asked Dr
Meller abruptly.

Leon opened his eyes wide. 'How do you know about
that?'

'The police confirmed your statement.'

Unlike Sister Susan, the doctor seemed to be speaking
earnestly. His words didn't sound patronising, but honest.

'You believe me?'

'Yes. A friend of yours, Sven Berger, was worried about
you and wanted to check on you. About a quarter of an
hour ago he found a man's corpse in your apartment.'

The stretcher came to a halt in front of some swing doors.
Leon lifted his head. 'And Natalie?' He tried to sit up. 'What
about my wife?'

*Has she been found too?*

Fear of the truth sealed his throat shut.

The doctor shook his head regretfully.

'I don't know. The police are trying to open a door, I
heard, but it's secured with a code.'

'A-Moll,' called Leon. 'Please tell them that the code is:
A-H-C-D-E-F-G-A.'

The doctor nodded and a telephone appeared in his right hand. It seemed he was on the line with the police, because he asked if they had heard Leon's last sentence.

'No, he can't be interviewed now, he's swallowed a battery and we need to pump his stomach,' said Dr Meller, trying to end the call. The person at the other end said something, and the doctor looked down at his patient with an expression of shock. Leon's heart stopped.

*Have they found her?*

'The investigator wants to know what happened to the other tenants,' asked Meller.

Leon's eyes widened. 'Oh my God, did that psychopath do something to them too?'

He thought of old Frau Helsing, who von Boyten surely can't have had anything against.

'No, erm . . .' The doctor wandered out of his line of vision, then appeared again on the other side of the stretcher.

'If I understood correctly, it sounds like no one's there.'

'No one? That's impossible. Ivana never leaves her apartment in the evening.'

'I'm afraid you don't understand.' Leon was pushed through the door into a tubular treatment room. 'According to the police, your neighbours didn't go out. They *moved* out. With all their valuables, cash and papers. All the house doors were open with the keys left in the outside.'

'What? But why?'

Dr Meller shrugged his shoulders cluelessly. 'I don't understand either, Herr Nader. But the police said the whole building looked like it had been evacuated.'

# Some months later

Somewhere in the world.
In a town you know.
Maybe even in your neighbourhood . . .

# 42

Dr Volwarth waited for his colleagues' applause to die down as he entered the conference room of the sleep laboratory.

'Thank you. Thank you very much indeed.'

He fiddled with the stud in his earlobe. Too much attention always embarrassed him.

'It's our joint success. You should be applauding yourselves.'

The group, two women and two men, laughed politely.

Only the chief doctor at the head of the table seemed disgruntled.

'It's a shame that any recognition will take a long time to come,' he interjected.

'You're right, Professor Tareski.' Volwarth's eyes flashed with bitterness. 'But we're not the only ones in the history of medicine to have risked their own well-being and freedom in order to achieve groundbreaking discoveries in the name of science. Just think of our colleagues in the Middle Ages, who were forbidden under threat of the death penalty to open the human body.'

He emphasised this statement with a raised index finger.

'Over thousands of years, doctors and scientists had to steal corpses from cemeteries for dissections, and often paid with their own lives for this desire to research. The Church was afraid that the lies in the Bible would come to light if people realised that Adam wasn't missing the rib Eve was allegedly made from. Back then it was the priests, and today it's other do-gooders who stand in the way of progress.'

The nurse by his side snorted with contempt and stopped stroking the cat on her lap for a short moment.

Ivana Helsing was getting on in years, but she was one of his most reliable helpers when it came to the careful implementation of experiments. And she had also introduced him to the von Boytens, for which Volwarth showed his gratitude with unconditional loyalty, even if she had a tendency to humanise the test subjects. Over time she had grown so fond of 'darling Leon', as she liked to call him, that in the end she had even pleaded for the experiment to be called off. Today she was happy and content that he had survived, even though Leon had not responded to her subliminal attempts to get him to leave the building. She hadn't developed any fondness for Natalie, on the other hand. Luckily. If you want to break new ground in the field of medicine, you can't be too sensitive. Subjects like Natalie and Leon, in this context, were nothing but animals in a laboratory. Whoever didn't have the emotional strength to take the loss of a chimpanzee had no place in the field of research.

'Anyone who carries out unapproved human testing must be prepared for contempt from the ignorant,' explained Volwarth in a self-congratulatory tone.

It was a vicious circle that his co-researchers knew only too well. Technically speaking, of course, the ethics of their profession required the approval of the test person. But sleep disturbances were anomalies of the subconscious. As soon as the test subject knew he or she was being observed, that changed the very behaviour that was to be investigated. No one slept in a laboratory like they did at home in their own bed. It was precisely for this reason that parasomnias were barely researched and the results gained in traditional sleep laboratories so inadequate. Tests provoking the violent excesses of sleepwalkers were considered unthinkable.

'By letting Leon Nader believe for an entire year that he was living in his own familiar environment, we were able to make groundbreaking discoveries in the field of somnambulism research,' said Volwarth proudly.

Three years of planning. From the selection of the subjects to preparing the laboratory: his deceased patient Albert von Boyten, who he had treated in his clinic until his death, had been the creator of unique architectonic masterpieces, which Volwarth had found to be excellent for his purposes. Distributed all over the globe, von Boyten's buildings had been constructed with secret levels between floors. The genius architect, a war child and Communist, had originally designed them as hiding places for the politically persecuted, but they were also excellently suited to being sleep laboratories. Beyond using them to observe the patients, it was also possible to expose patients to targeted stimulation.

The apartments were connected via secret passageways that could be accessed at any time, in order to get test materials in and out while the test subject was either elsewhere in the building or asleep.

The sleep phases which framed Leon's sleepwalking activities were luckily incredibly stable, as is often the case with patients with such disturbances. These created the necessary time windows in which the researchers could painstakingly prepare their experiments, for example copying the edited videos on to Leon's laptop. More complicated was the follow-up stage of the experiment levels in question. For this, Leon's apartment had to be returned to its original state; the wardrobe, for example (which was fixed with an electromagnet), had to be pushed back, the head camera hidden and the laptop turned off. For as soon as Leon awoke, nothing could be permitted to remind him of his nocturnal activities.

The deep-sleep phases were of such intensity that they had been able to undress and dress Leon, move him, and once even lay him in a bathtub.

Volwarth looked over at Ivana. On her lap, Alba was purring and pressing her little head against her mistress's hands so that she would start stroking her again. He couldn't help but remember the stubbornness of the old woman when she had insisted that they use an artificial but convincing fur mock-up instead of a real cat corpse for the experiment in the bathtub.

*And yet despite all the personal differences in the team, everything worked wonderfully.*

Not for the first time, Volwarth felt proud of himself and his team.

It had demanded a great deal of discipline, concentration and the precise implementation of the experiment procedure, but in the end all their efforts had been rewarded.

'Firstly, we have conclusively proved that intense mental trauma is able to provoke the complicated process of sleep-walking,' pontificated Volwarth.

They all nodded contentedly.

To start with, admittedly, they hadn't known how to actively put Leon into a sleepwalking state, but researching that was part of the experiment, after all. And just like the bacteriologist Fleming's discovery of penicillin, fate had played into their hands here too. Siegfried von Boyten had agreed to provide the house from his father's inheritance on the condition that he himself be allowed to participate in the experiment. Leon, in turn, had only been selected as a test subject because of Natalie. Volwarth's assertion to Leon that the hypnophobia from his childhood was so interesting that he still referred to it today was a lie. In actual fact, he had completely forgotten about Leon, until the day a colleague asked him for advice in a case where a patient was suffering from self-destructive sexual behaviour. When Volwarth encountered the familiar name of Natalie's partner while reading the minutes from her sessions, he instantly saw the potential for his experiments: a sleepwalker and a mentally fragile girlfriend. The perfect conditions to test if and what degree of psychological pressure could unleash sleep disturbances. It had been Volwarth who made contact with Natalie and offered help. Not the other way round.

'We have finally succeeded in proving the phase of sleepwalking to be an independent conscious state in which the patient is not just able to function and react, but also comprehensively communicate,' Volwarth continued.

He directed his colleagues to open the slim file in front of them on the table and look at the photo on the first page. It showed Leon Nader, clothed only in boxer shorts, standing in the corridor of the old laboratory.

'In this picture, our patient was already in the third stage.'

When Leon had woken up in his and Natalie's bed after drinking a bottle of wine alone the night before, he thought he was awake. But, in reality, he was in a highly stable sleepwalking phase that began with Natalie's flight and only ended once he went back in the bedroom and fell asleep again.

'In the subsequent conscious state, Herr Nader was unable to remember the events surrounding his wife's departure. He awoke in an empty bed and thought that she had left as a consequence of weeks of intense marital crisis. While he slept, we closed the wardrobe again and tidied up all the disorder. Given that Natalie had left him a goodbye note on the kitchen door before her abrupt departure, Leon was upset but not incredibly worried about her well-being, and therefore numbed himself with work for the days that followed.'

They had needed to remove the goodbye card in the first sleepwalking phases, of course, to ensure that Leon's mental torment was greater and his sleepwalking state more stable.

Volwarth smiled pensively.

No wonder Leon's friend and business partner was so confused. Sven Berger had experienced his friend in two different stages of consciousness, and according to whether Leon was awake or sleepwalking, the versions that he heard about Natalie's disappearance were completely different. First it was that Natalie was just taking some time out. Then that she had been beaten by him in his sleep. Leon, in turn, was unable to remember in his conscious state either his injuries or the camera, while during his sleepwalking phases he couldn't remember having taken his wedding ring to the jeweller's, giving his parents a cruise or that his friend had picked up the architectural model.

'It is really astounding how much we've learned about the sleepwalking phase,' said Dr Kroeger, who had joined the team two years ago as a neurologist and who was already flicking further forwards in the file.

'Just like when people are dreaming, a sleepwalker, too, remembers specific events from reality. But clearly, and this is the real sensation of our results, not everything. It seems that only intensely emotional events seep into the nocturnal memory.'

Volwarth nodded. This was exactly his hypothesis.

The miscarriage, Natalie's disappearance, the enormous pressure of his work deadline – Leon had been able to remember all of this. Less significant experiences, on the other hand, he hadn't.

But perhaps the most interesting thing, as far as Volwarth was concerned, was the fact that the sleepwalking memory could structure information in building blocks. This had been proven by the (incredibly difficult) staging of the first 'awakening': when Leon thought he woke up wearing latex gloves and the camera on his head, while in reality he was sleepwalking. From the moment he put the camera on his head the first time to his first viewing of the video tapes, fourteen hours passed. But fourteen hours in which Leon hadn't really slept, at least not exclusively. Firstly, with the camera on his head, he had fallen from the sleepwalking phase into an exhausted, almost comatose state, in which the researchers had been able to take the camera off him without any problems. Leon then slept four hours, woke up and worked on his model; a phase that he was unable to remember later when sleepwalking, and this was why he was so astonished when he realised during his phone conversation with Sven how much time had passed.

In order to prepare Leon for the next test, they added a light sedative to his tea. He drank it while conscious, which was why he soon went back to bed with a growing headache. With Leon in this numbed state, they had been easily able to put the gloves on him, as well as the camera on his head. The only thing they forgot was the watch he had been wearing during his last sleepwalking phase and which he'd taken off while awake as he worked. A discrepancy that Leon later noticed, but which luckily had no impact on the continuation of the experiment. Leon thought he was waking up after fourteen hours of sleep, but in reality he had suppressed the conscious phase in between, and his sleep-waking memory latched on – as they had hoped – directly to the point when he had ended his last somnambulistic phase: he got out of bed, looked at the video and discovered the wardrobe.

*All the rest is history. They would become world-renowned in the history of medicine!*

'The fact that we've been able to prove that a sleepwalking memory exists is phenomenal,' smiled Volwarth. 'And we've also learned that a patient clearly reflects on his state while sleepwalking.'

Volwarth was particularly proud of this result. Many of his colleagues – some of whom were here today – had doubted that it was possible to use external stimuli to penetrate the consciousness of the sleepwalker to the extent that he or she was aware of his situation but without freeing them from it. Yet this had been conclusively proven by the words and numbers Leon had noted on his hand in the experiment room.

'Look at this.' Kroeger held up a photo in which he was handing Leon a mobile phone in his living room. 'Nader was in the third stage here too. During our conversation he seemed absent-minded, as though under the influence of drugs, but he still appeared to take in everything I said to him. He could hardly look me in the eye, but he studied the photos we took of Natalie on the mobile phone in great detail. His speech was a little blurred, but he seemed stable otherwise.'

Volwarth nodded in agreement.

He had experienced at first hand how lasting Leon's imprisonment within the third stage had been.

At first the head camera had not been a planned component of their experiment. They had actually wanted to test with the prescription Volwarth made out to him whether Leon would leave the house during his sleepwalking phase. But by this point, he was already so convinced of his own guilt that he decided to hook himself up again of his own volition. As they hadn't been sure how precise his technical dexterity would be while sleepwalking, they had exchanged the camera he ordered for another, one that was easier to put together and install. In addition, this meant they could upload the manipulated videos on to his computer with the help of the switched USB sticks, without even having to enter the apartment.

Surprised by how adept their patient was, they had then tried out different levels of difficulty to test how strongly Leon was caught in the third stage and what physical and psychological achievements he was capable of during sleepwalking. From simple tasks like looking at pictures on a phone to the discovery of a combination of numbers on the thumbnail – in the course of the experiment, Volwarth had become more and more euphoric about Leon's abilities. He had even been able to solve the a-Moll puzzle.

'Sometimes I think our patient was clearer in the head than our team,' complained Tareski.

Volwarth nodded regretfully. 'I understand your chagrin, Professor, and I promise I'll be more careful next time with the selection of our assistants.'

'You certainly should be. It just wasn't possible to control Siegfried after a while, and he simply played out his own sadistic desires.' Tareski instinctively touched his neck. 'You shouldn't ever trust an amateur again with such an important task as the creation of the trigger footage.'

Volwarth sighed.

In truth they had wanted to find someone more reliable as bait for Natalie, but it had been difficult enough as it was to convince even one daring researcher to take part in their projects. And this time they had been searching for someone with relevant experience in a scene that was too hardcore for even S&M enthusiasts. When von Boyten Jr. unexpectedly offered himself for the task, they were incautious enough to accept due to desperation. It was clear to everyone that Siegfried just wanted to satisfy his own brutal desires, but didn't that make him pre-destined to provoke the kind of psychotic stress in Leon that they so urgently needed for their experiment to succeed?

And so it was von Boyten who offered the apartment to Natalie to reinforce their sexual relationship. It was the catalyst they needed to increase Leon's fear of loss to such an extent that he fell back into his old pattern of consciousness.

'The house belonged to him,' explained Volwarth. 'As you know, he threatened to expose the whole thing if we pulled him out of the experiment. I wish I'd had another option. He was our only weak point.'

They had given von Boyten a certain amount of freedom when it came to the contents of the tapes they played on Leon's laptop. The primary function of these recordings was to examine how defined the I-consciousness of the test individual was in the third stage, similar to the consciousness test carried out with animals to check whether they recognise themselves in the mirror or see their reflections as another creature. At the same time the recordings were intended to help discover to what extent the patient could draw logical conclusions from what he had seen.

The fact that von Boyten had climbed unauthorised into Tareski's apartment and almost strangled him to death with a shoelace had been neither planned nor foreseen. And especially not on a day when Volwarth was delayed, due to a presentation that could not be postponed, and therefore unable to step in.

'Even though you were the affected party, Professor, there was a positive outcome to the attack. The fact that Leon rescued you proved there's a sleepwalking conscience.'

Tareski didn't seem too convinced, but everyone else in the room nodded in agreement.

'And last but not least,' said Volwarth, trying to bring his summary to a conclusion, 'we almost succeeded, as a side benefit, in curing Leon Nader of his hypnophobia.'

The faked video footage had been designed to lure Leon into a labyrinth that seemed to lead down into the darkest passageways of his subconscious.

'For the whole of his life, our patient was afraid of falling asleep because he thought it turned him into a violent monster. The fact that he was able to overpower Siegfried von Boyten in the end meant that he overcame the trauma of his childhood. Now he knows that he doesn't hurt anyone when he sleepwalks, neither his loved ones, like Natalie, nor strangers like Professor Tareski.'

Volwarth smiled modestly and waited until his colleagues had stopped clapping.

'Before I ask you to turn to the last page in the file, I would like to take this opportunity to thank our generous donors. Without the Falconis, it wouldn't have been possible to finance our projects.'

The pot-bellied man of the couple that had inhabited the first floor of the old sleep laboratory smiled smugly, and yet Volwarth knew it was actually the elegant woman by his side who deserved the recognition. She was the wealthy one. For her husband, the experiment had been nothing more than cheap snuff-theatre, and if it was down to him he would have turned off the money tap early on, as soon as he became bored of it.

Volwarth sighed discreetly.

It was a shame that it was necessary to collaborate with such objectionable subjects, but there wasn't much he wouldn't do in the name of science. At least his donors had made an undisputable contribution to the success of the experiment by stopping Natalie's lift on the first floor and coaxing the young woman into their apartment, which was why Leon was so confused when she didn't come out of the lift on the ground floor. But this act and their money had been the Falconis' only noteworthy achievements, and

247

even their financial means hadn't been enough to cover all the expenses. Volwarth had even let Ivana talk him into flogging some of their research recordings to buyers on the internet. It made Volwarth feel sick when he thought about it, but with the money the project swallowed up there'd been no other option. Of course, he was neither able nor willing to lower himself to conversing with such questionable individuals, so he had left it to Ivana to send them the packages containing the tapes.

'I'm very pleased you're with us again today,' said Volwarth to the Falconis, gritting his teeth. Then he asked for the attention of all those present.

'Just like all of you, I regretted the fact that we had to leave our last laboratory in such a hasty manner. But with Leon managing to break free so unexpectedly, we were unfortunately left with no choice.'

Volwarth pulled four security keys, furnished with numbered bands, from his trouser pocket. 'Ladies and gentlemen, these are the keys to your new apartments. As always, you can choose the floor yourselves.'

He beckoned for his colleagues and sponsors to stand up and come closer.

The windowless room in which their meeting was taking place had a low ceiling, and Dr Kroeger had to lower his head as he went to stand beside Volwarth.

'On the last page of your files, you'll find a list with your new identities, as well as a rough overview of the planned series of tests.'

With these words, he pulled a black, opaque curtain from the wall, and a murmur went through the group.

'As I said, it's a shame we're no longer able to use our old space. But here we've been able to find even better conditions. And we'll still to be able to act incognito.'

He had begun to whisper, which was silly given that the

248

walls were adequately insulated. Noises could only penetrate into the laboratory space if they really wanted them to.

'Excellent,' said Kroeger in awe.

'Unbelievable,' Ivana agreed.

'Fantastic,' enthused Mr Falconi, for the wrong reasons.

The rest were silent, staring transfixed through the two-way mirror into the bedroom of the couple who were in the process of moving into their new apartment.

# 43

'It's unbelievable,' said the young man, putting a removal box down next to the bed.

'Isn't it, darling?' The woman, even younger, let herself fall back on to the bed with a suggestive smile. Her boyfriend followed her lead and kissed her full lips.

'I still can't believe we got our dream apartment.'

'Neither can I.'

He pushed his hand beneath her blouse and she giggled.

'It's wonderful,' he said, leaning towards her with a loving look.

'I know, isn't it?'

'I didn't mean the apartment.'

'Then what?'

'It's wonderful that you're smiling again at last.'

He kissed her, then said in a hopeful voice:

'I think everything's going to be OK again here.'

# Epilogue

It was impossible to make anything out through the material. Sven had tied the blindfold much too tightly. As soon as Leon took it off he would look like he had just woken up, with tired eyes and sleep creases on his face.

'Where are you taking me?'

He was holding on with both hands to the shoulders of his best friend, who in the last months had become his closest confidant. Numerous doctors had approached him, including prominent personalities, offering to work through the traumatic experiences of his recent past with him, but for obvious reasons Leon didn't want to have anything more to do with psychiatrists for the rest of his life.

'How much longer?' he asked impatiently. It was straining his nerves to stumble along blindly like this. Just a few weeks ago it would have been unthinkable to put himself in someone else's hands like this, but since they had moved into the new apartment he was making advances day by day.

'We're almost there.'

*You said that five minutes ago, when we got out of the car.*

The path sloped up gradually but steadily. Leon felt the sun on his face and heard music from the radio of a car driving past. His nose was itching, a sure sign the pavement was lined by blooming chestnut trees. The scent of warm asphalt was in the air.

'I hate surprises.'

'Then you'd better avoid your birthday,' replied Sven drily.

Leon thought about what they must look like. Some passers-by stopped their conversations, giggled and made silly comments ('What a lovely couple', 'Have fun, you two'), or whispered behind their backs as soon as they had passed.

Once Sven had led him around two more corners and then straight on for a long stretch, it seemed they had reached their destination, for they came to a halt.

'Finally.'

Leon moved to loosen the tight knot behind his head, but Sven took him by the arm.

'Stop, first I need to tell you something important.'

'What?'

'You won't like my present.'

'Excuse me?'

Leon blinked beneath the blindfold. Even more worrying than Sven's secretive behaviour was the fact that his friend had started to stutter again, albeit barely noticeably.

'They said it's too early, but I'm afraid it might already be too late.'

With these words, Sven pressed something into his hand that felt like a glass of hot water. Leon held it with the tips of his fingers so as not to burn himself.

'What the hell . . .?' He ripped the blindfold from his head and gaped at the object flickering in his hand. 'You're giving me a tea light?'

Sven shook his head. 'No. I'm giving you a vision.'

'Of what?'

'The truth.'

Leon obeyed the order to turn round, and almost let the glass fall.

A sea of lights danced in front of his eyes, fuelled by the numerous candles and tea lights that were arranged on a flight of steps.

'Is this supposed to be a joke?' asked Leon, wishing he had never taken off the blindfold.

The collection of letters, cuddly toys, flowers and pictures – some framed, but mostly wrapped in clear film – looked completely out of place. This was not the side of a street where some accident had taken place. They were not standing at the entrance to the home of some celebrity whose unexpected death was being mourned by their fans. Such a manifestation of collective grief belonged in the evening news and not at the entrance to the building from which Leon had fled, naked, on to the street, a few months ago.

'Why are you doing this to me, Sven?'

Some of the flames were extinguished and many of the flowers had wilted, which was no wonder considering the warm temperatures, but the wreath on the lowest step had been watered just recently. Drops pearled from the fir boughs, and the embroidered sash gleamed like new in the glistening sunlight.

*In deepest sorrow.*

Leon turned back.

Even his friend's eyes had filled with tears. 'I'm so sorry, Leon. But I think it's time you face up to the truth.'

Sven pointed at a framed photo in which Natalie was laughing directly into the camera. A photocopy with bleached-out edges. Like most of the portraits on the steps, it had been taken from a newspaper. Above it was the attention-grabbing headline:

Natalie Nader –
The Beautiful Victim of a Sadist

'But that doesn't make any sense,' whispered Leon.

*It's utterly impossible.*

They had found Natalie in the labyrinth. Without measurable vital functions. Siegfried had punctured her windpipe, torn her oesophagus. Her lungs had filled, at a torturously slow pace, with blood and secretions, every breath had brought her closer to the end. But as she was unconscious, Natalie's breathing had slowed down considerably, and this meant she did not immediately suffocate.

'She survived,' said Leon, throwing his tea light at the ground in anger. The glass shattered. The flame extinguished. 'They brought Natalie back to life!'

Once in the cellar, and once again on the way to the hospital. Even during the emergency operation, the surgeons had needed to fight time and time again against the flat line, but in the end they sent death back to the waiting room.

'She's alive!' screamed Leon, kicking several candles from the first step. Glass shattered, a frame broke.

'I was with her when she woke up!'

For several weeks Natalie had only been able to take in liquid sustenance, and her voice had changed. She didn't talk much, particularly not about what had happened in that building, but when she did, it sounded as though she was choking on something hot. Like the scars on her soul, the ones on her vocal chords weren't visible to the naked eye. Unlike the hollow above her larynx, which changed shape and became lighter when she swallowed.

'What's all this about?' asked Leon, holding in his hand a small crucifix that he had just picked up from the steps. In a rage, he threw it at Sven's feet. 'I had breakfast with her just two hours ago.'

*At our place. In our new home.*

'It's just a dream,' he heard Sven say, who was standing

at the foot of the steps. 'You're stuck in a dream and you need help to get out of it.'

'This is RIDICULOUS!' roared Leon.

Sven stretched his arms out towards him. 'Natalie is dead, you need to accept it. You're not living with her, you're living in a clinic. We have another fifteen minutes, then I need to take you back there.'

'You're lying.'

'If I'm lying, then why are you wearing pyjamas?'

Leon looked down at himself in horror. His legs were encased in thin pyjama bottoms, his feet were bare.

*No, no, no!*

He began to shake his head and didn't stop, like a child suffering from neglect.

'This isn't true. I'm not in the clinic any more. I live in, in . . .'

Leon looked at Sven helplessly, because he couldn't remember the address. It was a bungalow, without a cellar, without any neighbours.

*Without any tunnels.*

'Come on, you visited us last week. It's in the centre of town, and we have separate bedrooms because we want to take things slowly!'

*And at night, when the doors are closed, the windows bolted and the motion sensors activated, we take turns sleeping.*

'You're living in a dream,' repeated Sven. 'And now it's time for you to wake up.'

'Stay away from me.'

'I'm begging you, Leon. Don't fight it any more.'

'No, go away!'

'Leon, listen to me . . .'

Sven stretched his hand back out to him again. It was a blisteringly hot day and the midday sun was burning down, but Leon could feel nothing but cold.

'She's alive,' he cried, shivering and sinking down to the ground. 'Natalie's alive.'

Sven knelt down and grasped his friend's hands. 'I'm here, Leon. Look at me.'

'No.' Leon pulled his legs in towards himself and buried his face.

'LOOK AT ME!' screamed Sven, tearing Leon's hands from his face.

Then he hit him. Leon's cheek burned like fire. He gave Sven a tear-stained, furious look, and that was when it happened.

His friend began to dissolve in front of his eyes like wax on a warm hotplate.

His forehead stretched upwards and his chin became narrower. Cheekbones became defined where previously there had been only fat. At the same time his hair changed colour, becoming darker until it was almost the same shade of brown as his eyes.

'Wake up,' said Sven, who no longer looked like Sven and wasn't stuttering any more either. Instead, he was suddenly talking as though he had choked on something hot.

'WAKE UP!'

There was a crack. Loud and painful. Then Leon felt like he was being dragged into a suction pipe and pulled upwards.

He gave a start, flung his arms up, kicked around, then stamped the quilt to the foot of the bed and opened his eyes.

At first all he could hear was his own breath, then a soft voice whispered his name anxiously: 'Leon?'

He blinked. Warm sunlight, falling through the blinds, caressed his face. He was sweating.

'Can you hear me? Are you OK?'

A woman leaned over him, so closely that the subtle scent

of her favourite perfume filled his nose. A mixture of fresh hay and green tea. Over her larynx shimmered a scar that became lighter when she swallowed.

She stroked his cheek, then her smile disappeared and a familiar melancholy was reflected in her eyes.

'I heard you screaming and came across. Is everything OK?'

Leon nodded. 'Yes, everything's fine.'

He sat up and looked at the clock on the nightstand.

He reached up to his neck and touched his scars. Then, once he had gathered his thoughts, he spoke – still a little uncertain, like every morning – 'Don't worry, Natalie. I'm awake.'

# Acknowledgements

Early one morning at about half past two, having just finished writing the nineteenth chapter of this book the night before, I woke up my wife Sandra, who was sleeping next to me, and nervously asked her, 'Did you bring the baby back up from the cellar?'

Dazed, she answered, 'Have you gone mad?'

Then I woke up.

It wasn't the first time I'd done strange things in my sleep. I got married while I was asleep, after all.

Seriously, though. One time I started talking when I was wide awake, and then finished the sentence while I was asleep. First part: 'Tomorrow you'll have to remember . . .' Second part: '. . . not to put the pegs into the exhaust.' Something that baffled my wife just as much as my question about the baby which, in my dream, we were unable to save from whatever danger it faced.

I already described 'sleep paralysis' back in *Der Seelenbrecher* (*The Soul Breaker*) – that uncomfortable sensation where the mind thinks it's awake, but sleep is still holding the body captive. I don't suffer from it all that often, maybe once every two years, but when it does happen there's always a man in the room watching me, and there's nothing I can do when he raises his axe. I want to jump up, scream at him, at least try to signal for him to go for my wife, sleeping next to me, and not me – but all in vain.

I'm definitely in good company with this sleeping disorder. More than 20 per cent of the population suffer from similar symptoms. Of course, not all of us walk through the house, look for hidden doors or sleep-drive their cars to kill somebody like Kenneth Parks did; the case described in the book actually happened. But nonetheless many people sit upright, stare with wide eyes, and some of them talk nonsense like me. Others go into the kitchen, get dressed, write letters, have conversations with people who are awake, or even leave the house.

It's not a laughing matter. There's no way to protect yourself when sleepwalking. There's a much larger risk (and it's much more likely) that people will hurt themselves rather than do anything to harm others.

With that said, I want to clear up one thing – this isn't a work of non-fiction. The events occurring in this book are purely fictional, and any resemblance to living or dead people is, of course, unintentional and purely coincidental.

There is, however, a smidgen of truth in this fictional tale, just like there is in any good lie. The statements Dr Volwarth makes during his first conversation with Leon about sleepwalking are accurate. Research about somnambulism really is still in its infancy.

And let's be honest for a second. Are you 100 per cent sure you know what you are doing at night? If not, you could always go and buy a camera. But if you do, make sure you're alone when you watch the recording the next morning ...

Now, before thanking my wonderful team, who all possess the stuff dreams are made of (see the elegant transition I used there?), I'd like to give you, the reader, a virtual handshake. I'll admit it, I would still be writing even if I didn't have you.

An author is simply unable to suppress the urge. But it's a lot more fun with you around, and it also means I'm not forced to put a gun to my publisher's head so that he'll publish my book (but you should prepare yourself anyway, Hans-Peter, just in case the circulation dies down at some point).

I could recite the following names in my sleep, either because they've been with me from the very start or because I deal with them on pretty much a daily basis at Droemer Knaur. So, we've got:

Hans-Peter Übleis, Christian Tesch, Kerstin Reitze de la Maza, Theresa Schenkel, Konstanze Treber, Carsten Sommerfeldt, Noomi Rohrbach, Monika Neudeck, Patricia Keßler, Sibylle Dietzel, Iris Haas, Andrea Bauer and Andrea Heiß.

I hope I'll be forgiven for highlighting my editors Carolin Graehl and Regine Weisbrod in particular, as they suffer from an incurable, almost manic urge to improve books, and I always benefit from it. Also, the credit for the title goes to Carolin (much better than what I suggested!), so thank you for that as well.

If you should ever get the idea in your head that you might like to write a book, you're best off looking at your calendar right now and checking when you could to go to ground for a good few months without your family, employer or the police sending out search parties. You're also going to have to sort out someone to do all the work in the meantime (appointments, contracts, money transfers and red tape, organising readings and launches, and a great many other things ...). In short, you'll be needing someone like Manuela Raschke, but I'm not telling you her name.

You're also going to need someone to make sure you have a publisher in the first place – my literary agent Roman Hocke, who's worth his weight in gold, as well as his loyal co-workers Claudia von Hornstein and Claudia Bachmann from AVA-International, for instance.

261

Patrick Hocke, Mark Ryan Balthasar and my wife Sandra spent many a sleepless night working on my website, as did Thomas Zorbach and Marcus Meier from vm-people during all those times when I, once again, couldn't figure out the newest Facebook functions. But hey, all the curried sausages and warm beer I got you guys should be more than enough to say thank you, right?

Also, in case you're wondering why I always look so much better in my press photos than in real life, the answer has a name: Sabrina Rabow. My wonderful press agent always watches me like a hawk in public and makes sure I only ever show myself at my best. And my best can take a while to find!

As always, I'd like to thank my father Freimut as well as my brother Clemens and his wife Sabine for all the familial support they've given me. Their surnames are Fitzek as well! Crazy, I know.

And of course I can't leave out my long-term friends, confidants and accomplices: Arno Müller, Thomas Koschwitz, Stephan Schmitter, Christian Meyer, Jochen Trus, the amazing Zsolt Bács (who directed The Child so well and made the impossible possible), Petra Rode, as well as Barbara Herrmann and Karl Raschke, who gave me many a sadistic idea while on the treadmill (to clarify: I run, he stands next to me, whip in hand).

I'd like to thank all the booksellers, librarians and organisers of readings and literature festivals, without whom my books would have never found their way to you readers.

And I'd like to thank everyone who *didn't* ask me where I got the idea for The Nightwalker. I could say it came to me in a dream, but that would be a lie. All I know is that the idea captivated me to the point that I had to tell everyone nearby as soon as it was in my head. One of the first people who wasn't able to cover his ears in time when I told him, while we were having dinner with some friends, was Christian Becker. His production company Ratpack is responsible for some of the biggest German box-office success stories. He was immediately taken by it and commissioned Iván Sáinz Pardo to create a screenplay adaptation. Thank you so much, Iván, for all the inspiration your ideas gave me while I was still in the writing phase, and I'm really eager to see what the transition to film is going to look like, because one thing is certain – if the money does come in (always a bit tricky in Germany, after all), the book and the film will have to be somewhat different. And there's at least one twist in *The Nightwalker* that, in my opinion, is going to be impossible to transfer to the screen.

Speaking of opinions – you can reach me by email at: fitzek@sebastianfitzek.de and at www.facebook.com/sebastianfitzek.de as per usual.

Finally, before I forget, I really want to thank my wife Sandra, who always gives me her whole-hearted support. And who still hasn't told me if she brought the baby back up from the cellar, by the way. I'm going down there now to take a look for myself.

Wishing you dark dreams,

Sebastian Fitzek
Berlin, December 2012
In a (hopefully) conscious state

# About the Author

**Sebastian Fitzek** is the number one internationally bestselling psychological thriller writer from Germany. His unique mind-bending thrillers have sold over five million copies around the world and have been translated into twenty-nine languages.